Butterflies Swim In Light

Keith Harris

Published by Pending Press Ltd.

Butterflies Swim in Light
This third edition (the second full edition)
copyright © Keith Harris 2012

Butterflies Swim in Light
was first published in a much shortened form
with ISBN 1-903466-00
copyright © Keith Harris 1999
The second edition (the first full edition) of
Butterflies Swim in Light
with ISBN 1-903466-01
copyright © Keith Harris June 2000

All rights reserved.
No part of this book may be reproduced in any form without the
permission in writing from both the copyright owner and the publisher.

Cover illustration © Dafydd Davis-Hughes

All the characters in this novel are fictional,
any resemblance of these characters to living persons
is purely accidental.

This book is published by Pending Press Ltd.

ISBN 978-1-903466-02-5

A Note on this Edition of the Book

This novel was first published in 1999 in the form of an extract which included a Prologue and the first section of Part I up to *the Glutton's Tale*. The second edition (the first full edition) of the novel was published in June 2000 and also included the Prologue.

For this third edition (the second full edition) the Prologue has been removed, simply because it was conceived as the introduction to a whole series of novels and not to this one specifically. It bore in fact no obvious relationship to this book.
   Dream Choices was originally a chapter in Part II. This has been put as a short story separate from the novel into an appendix at the end of the book. Otherwise only a very light revision of the text has been made.

This book is dedicated to
Our Lady of the Butterflies

Butterflies Swim in Light

Part 1

1. Playing Angels

The new priest: Slender, thoughtful, blue-grey eyes, dark hair, medium height, mid thirties. My mother sometimes took charge of his household, we two tagging along to help or mostly just to play. I was seven, my sister five. Often he would spend time in prayer or meditation in the church. Sometimes we'd sneak in to peep at him. Mother told us a priest's first duty was to pray.

Once we crept in and saw him in one of the front pews, head resting on his hand and motionless. Napping for sure we thought. We stayed crouching at the back of the church for such a long time, maybe three or four minutes. Maria whispered we should play angels and wake him so he could get on with his prayers.

Tiptoeing toward him in the church's quietness, a couple of paces away we nudged each other and rushed up to him. He didn't flinch only slowly dragged his gaze away from the altar. Reluctance tracing through grey irises changed to a blue presence as he took hold of us, smiling at our surprised faces.

We nodded eagerly when he asked if we'd like to hear a story. Bending closer he promised in a whisper to tell us later about the wolf, the savage sad grey wolf.

As I pulled to the heavy church door my sister stood head hung, a breeze blowing light brown hair over her face. I stepped nearer and rested my hand on her shoulder blades. We were bathed in sunlight. Brushing aside waves of hair she reached up and touched my cheek with her fingertips, earnestly looking at me with those luminous brown eyes of hers.

Ray, do you think we chased angels away?
But we were angels too, weren't we?
Father Rufus wasn't asleep, was he?

I guess not. But he wasn't angry with us. Don't look so worried Maria, I don't think we did anything wrong. And, and soon we'll hear about the wolf.

Her face brightened in a twinkling. She tugged at my arm and went running down the steps, checked herself abruptly and turned back with an expression of primeval seriousness.

Do you think the wolf ate many people?

At her words I saw the slants of wolfish eyes, haunted and ravenous before me, and shivered. But my voice came out loud, *Last one to the kitchen pays a forfeit!*

We bounded off dodging between the apple trees.

2. Family Heirlooms

Right from an early age an authentic seriousness could transfigure my sister. She might be chasing around the garden then stop dead, almost as if touched by an unseen hand. The profundity riven in her features might be away as quickly as it came like the sun appearing for just an instant from behind clouds. At other times she'd wander thoughtfully over to me and blurt out an unbelievably dumb question or some saying cryptic with the spontaneous simplicity of a Chinese sage that'd just knock me sideways.

Once down by the lake, hardly more than a pond really but we called it the lake, I spotted some fish, many more than I'd ever seen there before. I tried to get a closer view, stepping carefully over large half-submerged stones and sometimes having to use my hands to keep balance in my slippery new Sunday-best shoes. I called to Maria to come see the fry before they scuttled out to the middle. She was gazing way off in the distance but walked over slowly toward me with a sort of puzzled look.

Ray, have you ever noticed how birds swim in air but butterflies swim in light?

My barely kept balance blew away with the light-swimming butterflies. Water came over my knees, my ass sliding down rough stone hit the surface and got slimed with cool green ooze.

Most of the way back we were laughing.

You should've seen your face Ray as your butt thrashed the water.

On approaching home we quietened down. We were not well off. My mother had been alone with us since before Maria was two. We had friends around church and were given lots of clothes but shoes, "Your own feet love your own shoes", my mother used to say. And she always brought us good well-fitting shoes no matter how much she had to sacrifice. I'd never known her buy a new dress for herself. Last weekend we'd gone into town and both me and my sister got brand new shoes. Mine weren't cheap.

Squelching back along the path I guess I knew they'd never quite be Sunday best again. Mother had come a little way to meet us. When she saw us, late for Sunday lunch and my behind not smelling of perfume – and the shoes! She lost her temper. I could see she wasn't so much angry with me as cut up because I wouldn't be able to look neat for the festival next week. Maria crestfallen by my side her tears dripping onto her own new shoes. My mother never beat us but now she was really bawling, *How could it have happened? Why?*

My eyes watering so much her face was only a wavy outline above me as I answered, *Because birds swim in air and Butterflies in light.*

What!?

I mumbled it again.

As my footing so her annoyance fled away with light-swimming butterflies. We told our story and all of us ended up laughing. Which stopped abruptly when mother put a hand to her mouth, *The pudding!*

We all flew back to the house but hardly on light or even air. Jogging along my trousers felt as if greased with soggy manure.

That saying about the birds and the butterflies became a family heirloom. Considering our home's lack of fineries I dubbed it and some other of Maria's crypticisms: the family heirlooms – verbals not jewels.

Whenever something untoward or surprising occurred, something which defied obvious explanation, one of us would put on a wise expression and solemnly announce, "It was because birds swim in air and butterflies in light."

This curiosity might have remained to gather dust in memory's treasure troves had not a strange thing happened that summer before leaving for college.

Walking alone through a clearing in the woods, a sudden sound of beating wings caused me to look up and see a blackbird making little cawings and flying erratically, very erratically but more or less in my general direction. Thinking I was about to be savaged by a rabid bird I thrust a hand up to ward off its coming attack and even thought about diving into the bracken.

The whole experience was a bit like reaching back to lean against a stone wall but instead of stern stone your hand melts into something cool and oily. The mind sways over emptiness as ordinary expectations topsy-turvy. Somewhere between dismay and utter non-understanding you turn around to see you've put your hand on a slug.

Only what I saw now wasn't a slug. In the instant of considering what evasive action to take, I noticed it wasn't at all intent on getting its claw into a defenceless human. The bird was chasing a butterfly.

Furiously beating bird wings, beak about to snap the gliding insect but the butterfly simply parted its wings and was away. It didn't flap, it just opened them and was gone. Only a little way off but in quite another direction to the flight of the bird whose momentum carried it past. Only a frantic swishing of wings brought it swirling round to couple again to the path of its prey. But before the beak could nip, the butterfly opened it wings and was gone.

The blackbird's wild threshing in the air lasted only a matter of seconds before it gave up the strain of the hunt leaving the butterfly to flutter serenely on about its business of sipping nectar from blossoms.

I gaped, it had been a bit like toying a cat with a ball on a string. The cat tries to pounce but before its claws strike, the string is jerked and the ball whipped away. The big difference though is that the ball is given a sharp muscular tug whereas the butterfly only opened its wings and was gone. Not flapping against the air, its movement in no wise jolting, just as if in the instant of being parted, its wings cuddled a rainbow and slipped through a warp in gravity, dancing on caressed light, or from the bird's-eye view: Polkaing cheek to cheek with a sunbeam.

The whole scene so intense and over so quickly left no time to conceptualise. The flustered momentum of the bird, the twinkling flight of the butterfly entranced me.

Then as the dawn chorus pervades a rosy sky words began to arise in my heart, "Because birds swim in air and butterflies in …"

I yelled, *Maria!* and ran so fleetly that I wondered if wings hadn't sprung from my ankles. My body wasn't so much bouncing along as flowing. I ran faster than ever before and without tiring almost without effort on and on. When nearly at our garden I glided into a walk, my breathing quick but not heavy, I wasn't out of puff and still elated.

My sister was sitting in the garden supposedly sighing over Latin grammar but from that expressive tilt of her head probably in Imperial Rome fondling a frightened lion in the arena of a crowded Colosaeum.

Stealthily as possible I closed on her from behind, just before reaching her I whispered her name. As she turned I lifted her under the arms, she was so light, and twirled her round in the air.

Well Missy Applecheeks, guess what I've discovered.
And I repeated the family maxim.

3. Elsewhere

Missy Applecheeks was a name I'd coined years and years ago on account of her not infrequent blushing. It wasn't often she really let herself go but if she did, it was almost like wringing cherries on her cheeks. Crimson went right into the roots of her hair and all down her neck. Once when she had a summer dress on I even saw her shoulders reddening.

Her general complexion, how shall I say, there wasn't much of anything general about her. General features? She had two eyes, a nose, mouth and, and well everything was kind of living. You've heard of the expression: Eyes are the windows of the soul. Well her countenance was 'eyes'. Everything about her face reflected how she felt. And just as people's faces light up when their eyes do, so Maria's whole figure shone when her face brightened or wilted if she felt sad.

Her general complexion? It was tanned in Summer, fair in Winter and red or white as the moods took her. It was seldom she really cherried up but little blushings could transiently appear about as often as most people scratch their noses.

With her rich imagination she'd often be elsewhere. Missy Elsewhere was another of my nicknames for her. She could be gazing in the distance and I'd creep up, tap her on the shoulder and ask, "Where's Missy Elsewhere today?" or, "Who's Missy Elsewhere wandering off with?"

And the degree of her reddening might offer some indication of the whereabouts of her elsewhereing.

We could all be sitting around the open log fire on a wintry evening not doing much of anything. I was pretty much of an elsewherer too. And so was mother, though looking back I'm convinced her elsewhereing was usually bound up with her past, reliving a regret or poignantly touched by some fond memory. I guess I elsewhered into the future, my own pretended future I suppose.

And Maria? Well, she just kind of elsewhered and it wouldn't unduly surprise me if much of her elsewhereing took place in spheres triumphant, that is, with the angels.

4. Sister Anna

There was this one time when Sister Anna, who read us stories about saints after Sunday morning Mass, found a book about angels. Guardian angels and the pains they get from their protégées – us wayward humans.

Sister Anna? She was a bit plump with a wide untroubled smile. When she looked at you, you kind of got the feeling you were about the only thing in the world that mattered to her just then. She was real old, forty or so. And when she put glasses on her nose to read, she became two round lenses on a round face.

She loved food too I'm sure because whenever one of the stories had a part dealing with eating or baking cakes or something, she'd put the book down on her knees and say, *Just think children ...*

And take us on an impromptu journey into the secrets of making bread or pressing grapes. We could all smell, almost taste the bread as it came out of the oven in her story. Or see purple grape juice gush over women's feet.

If the story were about a rich household we'd hear details about laying tables, see polished silver cutlery perfectly set around finest china, seasoning in the roasted meat would waft in our nostrils. In the book it might have just said, "They brought in the dessert." What the author didn't realise, but we knew because Sister Anna had told us, was that it was home made strawberry ice cream. We'd seen juicy red strawberries plucked and then piled in a mixing bowl, jugs of fresh cream and heaps of light brown sugar. We'd been in the kitchen of the storybook, watching the ingredients mixed up while surreptitiously pretending to nibble on an imagined strawberry.

When Sister Anna told a story it could sometimes be as though you were part of it. At the grand table the main meal over, the dessert coming round, dollops of strawberry ice cream would be ogling up at us from our plates, we'd all be waiting for the signal to dive in and indulge, when the maid entered, "Begging your pardon but beggars are at the door craving alms".

How did we feel? Probably just like the kids in the story, decidedly put out about those ugly beggar mugs keeping us from the ice cream. At this point Sister Anna would lean toward us and say, *Just think children ...*

And we'd be let into more secrets that the author of the story hadn't known. We'd hear how the beggars had spent their day. How they'd seen baskets of fruit carried past, juicy pears so close you could've just put your hand out and grabbed one. How they'd stood waiting at the kitchen doors of the wealthy, smelling apple pies bubbling in great black ovens ... and been turned away without a crumb. How they'd looked through a baker's window at warm bread and cakes being stacked, their stomachs turning over for lack of food and not a dime in their pockets.

Tears'd be rolling down everyone's cheeks as we heard about how one of the beggars was mercilessly beaten with staves for daring to pluck a solitary grape.

Our nun would pick up the book again and read on, "The poor beggars were pleading for food."

And us, how did we feel? We'd be looking down at our imagined strawberry ice-dessert and I wouldn't exactly say, if we'd really been there at that moment, that we'd have offered our ice cream to a beggar but we might have given away a third, even half of it maybe.

Sister Anna knew children and loved us.

5. A Muffin Meanie

Once she read us a story about muffins. Sister Anna's mouth-watering accounts of muffin making reigned supreme, nothing could have tasted so delicious. Only much later in life did I first bite into a muffin and then with endless disappointment for it wasn't at all like I imagined one of Sister Anna's to be. For years if anyone had asked what I'd most liked to have eaten for my birthday I'd have replied without the slightest hesitation: Muffins. Mother never made any. Good cook though she was, I think she realised she'd never manage to compete with the fabulous cuisine of our favourite nun.

Anyway in the story this little girl (who probably ended up being canonised) was given money by her stepmother to buy five muffins, two for the stepmother, two for her stepsister and one for herself. She'd walked to the baker's, seen steamy muffins placed in a bag and gone out into the chilly air without so much as nibbling a crumb. In the frosty street was a poor waif selling matches who looked so cold and hungry. Quick as lightning she drew a still warm muffin from the bag and gave it to the match-seller girl. On reaching home and having to explain why there were only four not five, she simply answered she'd already taken hers.

First the stepmother beat her for not waiting to eat with them. Then the stepsister pulled her hair and kicked her because she'd eaten the biggest muffin for sure. Then the stepmother smacked her again because they'd taken so much time beating her and bawling her out that their own muffins had gone stone cold. Finally the girl was made to sit in a draughty corner of the room with a glass of water while the stepmother and daughter drank hot creamy cocoa and chobbled muffins by the fireside.

The girl was sent off to bed. Kneeling in the cold and dark beside her bed she whispered prayers. Instead of asking God to make the stepmother puke her guts up or send cockroaches to crawl under the stepsister's bedclothes, tears just rolled down her cheeks as she begged Our Lady to keep the little match-seller snug and warm.

Looking back the story didn't ring true, at least not the last part. After all if a little child could endure all that and not feel a touch of resentment she was certainly no saint but already an angel with no need to come down and live here among us tramps. I would have wanted to punch the stepsister smack in the nose and wished for a troop of two-toed imps to have chased them both down into a freezing cellar for the night.

But that first part – Sister Anna's long preliminary prologue about muffin making and the devastating possibility that a human hand could have given away an ambrosial muffin, given away such manna to some bitchy little orphaned match-seller – that might have been possible, could just perhaps have been authentic.

(I always remember Rab's statement in a London pub that time the three of us, Rab, Rol and me, were travelling on Eurorail. We'd gotten down half a dozen pints each and were about ready to keel over. Our early boisterous talk dampened as closing time approached. One of us mentioned 'authentic' in some or other context. Pain crossed Rab's face as he passed his dark-skinned hand over his forehead and through his close-cropped fuzzy black hair. Then suddenly he'd slammed a fist down on the table causing beer to slurp from one of the glasses. Tears were in his eyes as he gazed across the smoke-filled bar and in a quiet voice said, *Authentic, that's a word that makes your inside want to cry.*

All three of us stared down at half-empty pints, speechless before daunting authenticity of 'authentic.')

Today it would take something big, something like digging limbless survivors from a train wreck, for an outer event to implode such emotional shock waves in me as that muffin handout did then.

Trudging back along our path through the woods, the leaves still wet from early morning rain, I kept seeing before me the girl's hand giving away her only muffin and the weeny cold hand of the match-seller's taking it.

It shattered me that anyone could have given away a muffin, a warm heavenly muffin, just given the only one she had away. Shaken body and soul I lifted my face abjectly to the clouds about to utter something like, "Dear God please don't expect me to give away muffins."

I imagined myself hiding behind a tree and shouting out in shame and misery, "God, it's not fair, not fair to ask a person to give away his muffin, his very own muffin!"

Yet as my eyes rose skywards, words sort of sank back in my throat. Even though I was young then, (it must've been a year or more before Father Rufus came) the idea of troubling the Heavenly Father that untroubled Sunday for the sake of muffins struck me as suddenly very dumb. Muffins, I guess, don't cut a big deal up there.

Maria had been tripping along beside me. Sometimes skipping and singing softly to herself, now and again eyeing sort of curious her brother in his agonising.

She was humming to herself. Probably she'd have happily given away the darned muffin. Unlike her brother who was always hungrily awake at mealtimes she could as easily elsewhere over a banana split as over a log fire. It might not even have seemed surprising to her that little Miss Santy Pants hadn't started to holla for a throng of three-clawed imps to terrorise her step family. Sometimes I really did think my sister spent half her time with the angels.

Back home I left Maria in the garden, charged upstairs, brushed away a tear of resentment, dumped myself down on my bed and began to picture Our Lady. It didn't seem at all strange to me then that I could simply open a vivid impression of her in my mind and moan numerous gripes to her.

Hunched up stubbornly on the edge of the bed, chin in hands looking down at the (imaginary) blue of her dress and grumbling about how unfair it was that God should expect someone to give away his muffin, his only muffin to some snotty little orphan match-seller.

Mm, she said (or 'mm' I imagined her saying).

I glanced up into her deep kindly eyes smiling and concerned at one and the same instant. Brown, I think they were, a bit like my Maria's; except that my Maria's eyes could look timid when it was dark or when listening to a very scary story about goblins or spooks or something. Then she'd huddle closer up to me. I always felt happy, noble almost when she did that. I was so pleased my sister trusted me. Sometimes at night she'd come into my room calling my name softly and settle into bed beside me. She wouldn't say she was scared but I could feel her shivering and not just from cold. If I'd been lying awake by myself in the dark every little creak and scrape would have made me numb. But with her warmth near me little scratchings seemed far off. We'd whisper and tell stories together. If she fell asleep I'd pretend to be an Arthurian knight in full armour standing guard beside her, a damsel sleeping at the edge of a great and sombre forest. Or maybe we'd pretend to be children lying under think furs in a mountain cave. Beside us Maria's teddy bear grown to huge proportions our protective friend.

But back to the (imagined) figure smiling down at my muffin morbidity, goblins or dragons wouldn't have got much change out of this little lady's eyes and as for two-toed imps they'd have scampered wildly back to their two-tunnelled holes.

My Maria's eyes could get perplexed about some natural happening. I mean she could understand that spiders play web-spinning especially on days before frosty nights so shimmering white nets of gossamer appeared next morn. But she just couldn't get the idea that they spin webs to trap flies. Instead she'd make up rambling stories like the fly was cold and jumped into the web; the spider's wrapping her up to keep her warm and in an hour he'll set her free again. Or the spider's spinning a wedding dress for the fly so they can get married on the morrow. She'd even go as far as to make up little tunes and rhymes:

>The spider's going to marry the fly
>Marry the fly, marry the fly.
>The spider's going to marry the fly
>Hi, hi, marry the fly.

I gave up trying to initiate her into murky motives of crawling things.

I could be telling her some fact about nature's everyday struggle for survival when tears would well up in her eyes. I'd trail off with a phrase like, *Well, just some people say swallows are gobbling gnats as they swerve about up there but perhaps they're just having a ball.*

She'd frown for a few seconds. Then bubble up with something such as, *You know swallows are black and white just like those Welsh collies, the sheepdogs we saw in that book. So maybe swallows are gnatbirds I mean like sheepdogs they might be gnatsheepdogbirds swooping around to keep the gnatsheep in their pens.*

I'd look down at her, my perplexity meeting hers. But I just couldn't stand to hurt her so I'd say nothing about the possible identity or non-identity of the gnatshepherds. I'd only shake my head and sigh, *Gee, it must be a hard life for those gnatsheepdogbirds with all those gnatsheep just aching to jump their air fences ... come on let's go play.*

While my Maria's eyes could perplex and cloud about a helluva lot of things. This Maria (the one imaginatively looking down at me), definitely this little lady's eyes knew a thing or two. Maybe even the identities of the gnatshepherds, the owners of the Welshswallowcollie-gnatsheepdogbirds,who knows?

Only she must have her work cut out, must be as busy as those gnatsheepdogswallows keeping the gnatsheep in their air pens, as she rushes around to kids like me sulking over mishandled muffin-handouts and other such tragedies of growing up.

I was saying to her, *God shouldn't expect a person to just hand over his hard-earned muffins to some crummy little muffin-demanding orphan street-shark.*

Mm, she said (or 'mm' I imagined her saying). Then she suggested, *What about Maria?*

Only this I didn't imagine. I mean I had a good feeling about what I imagined in my imaginations and I'm sure as hell sure – oops! I mean sure as heaven sure I didn't imagine her saying that in my own imagination. I mean she must've imagined it herself, she must've imagined her words into my imagination. That is, I swear I didn't imagine what I heard. I just heard it, heard it directly, directly, that is, in my imagination.

My jaw dropped, *What?*

At least I think I said it aloud but maybe I just said it aloud in my imagination.

Anyway to cut a long story short after she'd said, *What about Maria?*

And I'd said, *What?*

She said, *Would you have given the muffin to Maria?*

I looked up to Our Maria with as much consternation as I've so often looked down at my Maria.

A tapping interrupted our conversation (our imagined conversation) a head peeped from behind the door. It was Maria, my Maria and not in my imagination, she was looking pleased.

Ray, I've picked apples for us.

She strode in beaming, holding up two apples and handing me the biggest and most ripe, taking the meany one herself. I grabbed the little one just as she set her teeth to it.

That one's mine, this is yours.

I turned slightly and winked at Our Maria – or winked to where she would have been standing, would've been standing, that is, in my imagination.

And I imagined or felt I could have imagined her nodding and saying with a knowing smile, *Good, first learn to give muffins to Maria and then when you come of age, you'll be able to hand out muffins to every sneaky, snidy, dirty, muffin-grabbing little orphan pickpocket street-mugger, you meet.*

Quite some woman Our Lady – did you ever meet her? I mean did you every imagine meeting her. I mean did she ever imagine herself into your imagination meeting you meeting her?

Feeling the moral glow of a muffin-giver I bit into my apple. Sour as sour! I glanced over at my sister as I tried to chew. Her face looked as though someone had squirted freshly pressed lemon juice between her lips.

Er, delicious Maria, how's yours?

F-fine.

You know what?

What?

Apples are good for the garden.

Really Ray! Mm, the garden hasn't had it's dinner yet, has it? Do you think we could feed apples to it?

Sure.

We ran over to the window and tossed the apples out.

Then this newly accepted member of the apple-givin' club walked hand in hand with his sister down to Sunday lunch.

6. Angel Stories

Half a year or more after that muffin business the group of us kids at church graduated from saints to angels when Sister Anna came up with a book about our winged protectors. In a Catholic upbringing you kind of get acquainted early with the notion of angels but until she read to us from that book. I'm sure I never gave much thought to what it might really mean to have an angel, my own guardian angel.

Only because of what happened after Sister Anna left suddenly and never returned. Something dark came between me and that time. I guess I blotted out the memory of most of that year before Father Rufus arrived. So the immediacy bubbling through her angel stories didn't become a part, not a conscious part at least, of my way of opening up to life.

It isn't long since I first made the effort as an adult to cut through that period when M66 interrupted our childhood and sought to relive what Sister Anna's angels brought us.

These tales were with us from early in the new year until June and shared common patterns of construction. Each was read over two or three Sundays. If I remember aright the person was usually but not always a man or boy while the angel or 'angeline' was feminine.

We'd follow someone together with his angel through a day's events. Then we'd see him asleep while his angel suffered and sat wondering how she could help her charge to open his heart to penitence and change. Next day would bring about events which forced him to make choices.

But to try to clamp abstract structures on her stories is a bit like trying to gain an impression of a person's feet from the brand name of their shoes. Her stories were alive.

Her stories? Yes, you know I've scanned databases in the Library of Congress and used internet search engines but have never been able to trace these tales. Thinking back there seemed a concentration over her reading of them and an absence of impromptu digressions that I wonder if they might not have been hers. Her own attempts to make up angel stories for children.

Maybe the best I can do is to retell one from memory. Alas, I cannot conjure up Sister Anna's inimitable voice. The style is mine not hers.

And the more I tried to regain a picture of Aroldaccio (pronounced Arollaccio) the more he took on a life of his own. Once me and my sister made up stories together about him and maybe elements from these in metamorphosed guise have intruded. I am now in my forties. Somehow the original Aroldaccio tale seems to have grown up too but slower than me. Sister Anna told children about him. An adolescent jocularity spills over his story as I rediscover it today. But perhaps this only goes to show there is life in that character she brought to us.

For extraneous elements not in her original I hope Sister Anna (and the reader!) will pardon me.

7. The Glutton's Tale

Aroldaccio is in his twenties and heavy. His bulgy cheeks glisten with beads of sweat at the mere mention of edibles. His wide mouth can open like a hippo's, his earlobes hang in a blob. His upturned nose, blue eyes and nigh colourless eyelashes give his face a piggy look. He is a giant among eaters and very large of proportions.

He likes people but more than anything he adores and constantly gorges himself on food. All kinds: Roasts, juicy steaks, fish, potatoes, chips, corn on the cob, rice, tortillas, curries, sweet and sour, hot and spicy, fruit, ices, chocolate – you name it, he eats it. And the heavier the food the better he likes it.

Where an ordinary person might take a slice of bread or a roll with their meal. He devours a family loaf or two, biting off great chunks of bread to rival in size a heavyweight champ's fist. Between bites he ladles soup into his mouth.

Nearly every morning he is woken by his own snoring. Sometimes his snores remind him of a food blender or a gurgling bubbling stew. To his half-awake senses his snores sometimes seem to sizzle like a huge frying pan full of ham and half a dozen double-yoked eggs.

A lover might awake reaching out with listless sighs for his beloved. Aroldaccio usually comes to consciousness trying to grab hold of dream-picture food. He blinks when he realises where he is. At first he feels downright cheated because his dream-food isn't real food. Then a smile curls on his lips as he chuckles naughtily to himself, "A whole day! A whole day in front of me to eat food in!"

In a trice he's thinking of buttered toast while his feet automatically take him to the larder. Generally though he doesn't have time to make food only to eat it.

A wealthy Swedish uncle set up a trust fund for him providing a regular income big enough to keep a family of six in luxury. It just about covers his basic diet. He makes extra money by entering eating competitions. He's the State Champ.

On average about once a month one or other of the city restaurants organises an eating contest on a one-to-one basis: Aroldaccio versus a pretender. Usually somebody driven in from a neighbouring state. As these matches provide the extra cash needed to satisfy his gourmand desires he generally takes them pretty seriously, by fasting for about half an hour before they start.

His encore is to polish off what remains on the plates of a defeated and groaning rival. Whatever else one might say of him, he really does love his victuals.

When he was young, Aroldaccio's angel shimmered with colour and beauty. But as he grew older (and heavier) she wasted away. As one by one his friends turned away from him (he only paid visits to eat their pantries bare) all joy left her.

She is no longer able to share in spiritual community and has become blind to the surrounding heavenly worlds. All around her is darkness. Only as through a tiny opening of light high, high above her is she able to glimpse the Throne and catch echoes of the highest hierarchies praising the Trinity.

She guards, cherishes, protects, visits and defends her beloved Aroldaccio ... yet all he cares about is the food he puts in his gob and is able to taste from his pallet right down to his intestines.

She has lost her power to speak.

When their protégées roam the worlds of sleep most guardian angels can whisper or sing and inspire their charges to follow ideals. But she only sits beside Aroldaccio silent and pale as he snorts and rolls on his bed dreaming perhaps of gigantic jellies and buckets of milk shake.

It so happens one day that the Queen of Angels (who is Our Lady and who looks after her angels as our guardian angelines care for us) gazes upon Aroldaccio's angel and takes pity on her. She sends St Michael to her.

The mighty archangel stands silently beside Aroldaccio's angeline. But she is unaware of his presence. Tears flood from her as she raises her sight to the Highest and begs help for her treasured Aroldaccio.

He isn't aware of any of this, snoring like a motor mower he lies restless in the foetal position, legs tucked up, dreaming he's wrestling with a giant chocolate rabbit and biting off a chocolate ear.

St Michael casts not even a disdainful glance down on the slumbering snoring shape. But as his angel pleads mercy for her protégé, the archangel lifts his radiant wings. And is in a higher heavenly sphere beside one of the Father's archai. St Michael and the archaiel (a countenance with wings) look down upon the suffering angeline. The archaiel steadies his wings – and is before a throne of the Father. A moment later (because time in the spiritual heights is not like down here) the archaiel is beside St Michael once more. And brings a message.

"His doom awaits him."

St Michael nods. And descends.

His descent cuts off the angeline's vision of the Highest and allows her to see him. He takes her hand, raises her up, his archangelic radiance about her as he draws his sword. St Michael speaks not a word but with his sword he points. The angeline follows his stern glance ... and glimpses Aroldaccio's coming day.

Oblivious to the deeds of night Aroldaccio wakes with a pillow in his mouth believing it to have been a deep-pan pizza.

Today will be no ordinary day in his life for a crossing of destiny is rapidly approaching. His feet take him down town to the quarter with Latin cafés and restaurants.

Giuseppe a plump and moustachioed Sicilian is standing outside his eating joint. *Omaccio mio!* he calls out loudly on catching sight of Aroldaccio. And escorts him in, *A pizza on the house, Marina, for our celebrity.*

There are quite a few customers. A distant cousin of Giuseppe's, a swanky Italian with greased back hair who's just arrived back from a stint in Europe, is entertaining at the bar with stories about the old country.

He has also won five dollars from many of those in the café. The wager: to eat two average-sized square cream crackers (the dry kind you eat with cheese) within a minute. No liquid is to be taken while you're chewing and the biscuits have to be completely swallowed. You think it's easy. So did the people in the café and many of these are five dollars poorer. The one recently returned from Europe has already taken over fifty bucks.

Giuseppe, whispering in Italian to his distant cousin not to start before he returns, introduces Aroldaccio then goes out darting from an Italian trattoria to a Spanish bottega, to

Mexican fast-food take-away, to an Argentinian steak house ... to tell them the State Champ has arrived. Apparently the bet has become known all down the street. Latin gossip travels faster than a forest fire in a gale.

The distant cousin winks to the other clientèle as he starts to explain the bet.

You have to realise that more than a quarter of an hour has elapsed since Aroldaccio last ate and that was only a big bag of popcorn so he's peckish. And when he's hungry he has trouble focusing his attention on anything but food.

The distant cousin explains the nature of the bet and puts two cracker biscuits down on the bar. Aroldaccio doesn't comprehend. He thinks the guy is asking him to pay five dollars for two biscuits.

Five dollars for two crackers? shaking his head in disbelief.

No Aroldaccio! interjects Marina who works in the café. *If you eat two crackers he'll pay five dollars to you!*

She taps him on the chest with the back of her hand. Aroldaccio shakes his head in even greater disbelief. He just can't take in how anyone in their right mind would give him five dollars for eating two crackers ... but he begins to reckon: Five dollars is enough for three large pizzas plus the one on the house makes four. In his fantasy he sees a table with four pizzas in front of him, una Napolitana, una Quattro Stagioni, una ...

Marina's voice interrupts his day-dreaming, *Will you take the bet?*

The distant cousin puts a five-dollar bill beside the cream crackers. By now Giuseppe has returned with most of the Latin quarter trying to crowd in behind him. Giuseppe places a fiver of his own on the bar.

Go for it omaccio!

Aroldaccio pops the two crackers in the cavern called his mouth. After 15 or 20 seconds he stretches and yawns, his mouth is completely empty.

The distant cousin takes it in good spirits, *Always somebody can do it*, smiling and still fifty bucks better off than when he arrived.

But Giuseppe has bigger things on his mind. Nudging the winner with his elbow.

Tell me, Aroldone, how many crackers could you eat, eat like under the conditions of the bet?

Five. He answers without thinking.

The distant cousin's eyes light up, *Five in a minute?*

In half a minute.

Five of those crackers in half a minute without liquid intake?

Aroldaccio nods, *Yeah*, and looks longingly over to the pizza bubbling in the oven.

The distant cousin can feel a wad of other people's greens in his fingers (but as they say in the Old Country: Greed riseth before a de-fleecing).

Fifty bucks says you can't.

Giuseppe turns up his lips as he carefully eyes his cousin (fourth removed on his great uncle's side) *I'll cover that and raise you another fifty*. Giuseppe has never lost a bet on Aroldaccio.

Now there's a hundred bucks, more than the distant cousin's winnings, riding on the five crackers. But this is only the beginning. Behind Giuseppe a whole crowd of Latins: Mexicans, Spaniards, Italians, South Americans, are taking out their wallets. Five-dollar, ten, twenty-dollar bills are riding on Aroldaccio's puissant organs of digestion.

Nobody has ever lost a bet on Aroldaccio.

Not even when the city newspaper imported 'the Beast from New York State' for a steak-eating competition. Nor when 'the Gorilla-Man from the Borneo Jungle' came for a fruit gnashing contest.

It would probably have taken a great white shark to have out gorged Aroldaccio in his prime.

Marina's writing down who's betting what. Giuseppe shouts for quiet and asks his cousin how much he can cover ... with European travellers cheques: 360 bucks. Quite a lot of money back in those days.

A frantic rush ensues among the Latins to place their bets with Marina before the ceiling is reached.

In the commotion a gentleman pushes forward from the back of the café. Late fifties, greying hair, distinguished in a rugged sort of way. He is the owner of a couple of betting shops; gambling is his livelihood. He is tempted, very tempted to cover excess bets because he doesn't believe anyone, not even our celebrity guzzler, can munch and swallow five cream crackers in thirty seconds. But something holds him back.

All his life he has lived by a motto: Never bet on human strengths only on human weakness. And over the years he has gained a cunning eye for people's failings. As he grew older he turned away from gambling's knife-edge excitement to the security of the certain bet.

Christened George Macgreedy, his father was a proud and illiterate Scot named Macreedy (there'd been a slip on the son's American birth certificate). His mother was

Mexican. Everyone in the Latin quarter knew him as Sir Giorgio.

Aroldaccio's grandeur is his digestion, so being true to his motto, Macgreedy refrains from direct involvement. He has always enjoyed being a fly on the wall especially when human foolery comes to the surface in crowds. He is standing now arms folded, back against the wall to observe.

The feverish conversing around him has gone on in a mixture of Italian and Spanish, in spite of his Latin-sounding name Aroldaccio speaks neither. His mother being a strapping Swedish blond, the father he hardly remembers, an Argentinian, a one-time elephantine centre forward turned third-rate American football player.

Aroldaccio came into the café expecting pizza. The pizza is blackening in the oven and nobody cares.

Marina calls a stop to the betting. Dollars are piled up on the bar. Everybody suddenly goes quiet. All eyes focus on the massive Aroldaccio who points to the oven and mumbles, *Pizza.*

Pizza, bizza, basta, mutters Giuseppe. *Crackers, five crackers! You can eat them all in half a minute, no?*

No?

No? Yes!

Yes.

Yes or no amico, can you do it, yes?

Yeah.

No drinking and all the crackers down in the gut, thirty seconds, okay?

Okay.

Aroldaccio reaches for the packet. His arm is grabbed by the distant cousin who then counts out five crackers carefully placing them one on top of the other. Aroldaccio reaches for the crackers.

No, first the watches!

After some delay and much Latin shouting, two stop watches are brought in. Aroldaccio's mind has already left all noise and disturbance around him. He is completely focused upon the crackers. He likes dry biscuits, he likes any kind of biscuits, maybe even dog biscuits.

Like a hound straining on the leash to follow the hunt Aroldaccio's jaws and inner jowls are aching to close on the cream crackers.

He has them in his hand now. The distant cousin holds his forearm as countdown begins.

10,9,8 ...

Aroldaccio often swallows. Whenever he thinks of food his mouth waters. Since he is always thinking of food he is constantly salivating, constantly swallowing.

Now as he beholds the cream crackers saliva secretes into his mouth at a rate to match milk flushing from a dairy cow's distended udder. There must be a good half cup of spittle in his mouth as countdown nears completion.

3, 2, 1, zero!

Aroldaccio tilts his head back slightly and gapes like a hippo, the five crackers slide in at one go. The rate of salivation on exponential increase.

Within ten seconds he's sucking his teeth. A couple of seconds later he opens his mouth, clean as tooth-brushed. Wild cheering erupts around the café. A couple of young bloods try to lift him and rick their backs in the process.

Aroldaccio's features become mournful, his nostrils are aware of burnt pizza. Badly cooked food saddens him in the way most people are cut up by the sight of human or animal suffering.

Half the Latin quarter accompany the distant cousin to the bank to cash his European traveller's cheques. The other half stay milling around Giuseppe's café praising the cream-cracker champion.

Giuseppe suddenly remembers a letter which came earlier for Marina. He hands it to her. She opens it nervously, clenching the paper tightly as she reads. Then she lets out a wail trailing off into sobs, *Mia, Giuliana, mia Giuliana*, and sinks to her knees.

Her bright-eyed ten year old daughter Giuliana hobbles in from the kitchen. One of her legs is a bit shorter than the other and seems a little deformed. The result of a road accident. She was knocked down by a hit-and-run driver a couple of years earlier. The doctors say it will get worse as she gets older unless she is able to undergo a series of specialist operations. The cost $5000, a big sum back in those days. And in God's own country a lot of people like Marina and Giuliana aren't covered by insurance schemes.

The letter is a reply from an appeal by Marina to a charity foundation. It declines politely to make any contribution toward Giuliana's opps.

Aroldaccio forgets even food for a while as he looks down at the sobbing Marina holding tightly on to her daughter. Somebody in the café calls for quiet. The speaker is about average height, could be of virtually any age and probably of Northern European stock but he speaks Italian with a perfect Florentine accent. (It transpired later that nobody ever saw him before and he never appeared in the district again after that afternoon.)

I propose a wager. Sir Giorgio over there can cover it. If we win we'll get our money back and the winnings will go to Marina for her daughter's operations. The bet is: Aroldaccio fasts for twenty four hours! What do you say Sir Giorgio?

Macgreedy is rapidly calculating: Aroldaccio's strength is his eating, his weakness ... the bet was as good as won, near certain ... but should he lose then Giuseppe's Sicilian connections would make it extremely inadvisable to default on the pay out. The near certain needed to be very certain ...

The speaker looking intently at Macgreedy, *What do you say Sir George?*

Macgreedy glances across at Aroldaccio's large presence slobbering and swallowing as he gazes with a lover's yearning at the oven.

A smile of triumph is visible on Macgreedy's face as he answers, *A 48-hour fast and I'll give odds of 2 to 1.*

Aroldaccio would never be able to hold out for two days and two nights. Macgreedy's sure of that. He has always placed his bets on human weakness ... and now he is the owner of a couple of swollen Swiss bank accounts.

The one who proposed the gamble counts out a hundred bucks on the bar and turns to the people in the café, *That's on Aroldaccio for Giuliana!* He raises a clenched fist, *Come on, friends, think of Giuliana, you get your money back and Sir Giorgio pays double for Giuliana. And he can well afford it!* casting Macgreedy a pointed look. *Come on, friends, come on, remember no one ever lost a bet on Aroldaccio!*

The Latins go for their wallets again, money is handed to Giuseppe who makes a list of who's given what.

Macgreedy can already smell greenbacks flicking through his fingers. His favourite saying has always been 'A fool and his money ...'

A vociferous debate ensues about the conditions of the contest (Aroldaccio against himself) where it is to take place, when it is to start. It is finally agreed it will happen here in Giuseppe's café.

Fasting in a café! chuckles Macgreedy to himself. Aroldaccio will be allowed water: tap water, sparkling or still mineral water, any kind of water but nothing else. The event is to begin in eight minutes, from three o'clock Wednesday afternoon to three o'clock Friday.

There is only one slight problem, as all the talk has gone on in Italian, nobody has yet told Aroldaccio ... and he still thinks he's come in for a pizza.

(Sister Anna would have left off the telling at this point. We'd have gone off wondering if Aroldaccio would agree to the bet and if he did would he get through it, would Giuliana get her opps – and would his angel regain the power to sing to Aroldaccio? We'd have had a whole week to ponder such questions. And in the pondering ... well, Aroldaccio has somehow become as real to me today as many a kid I met during my school days.)

Aroldaccio came in for a pizza or so he thought. So far he's seen a burnt pizza deposited in the bin and if you discount the seven cream crackers, not eaten for over an hour.

The conditions of the contest all but agreed, The arguing dies away, the decibel level plunges toward zero. Everyone looks over at the big guy.

One problem left, says the man who first proposed the bet, *He has to agree.*

All eyes are on Aroldaccio. Everybody there is hoping he'll go for it, is willing him to take on the bet.

He points nervously over to the oven and blathers, *Pizza.*

Pizza, fizza, frizza, fresh air! Fresh air, amico mio, fresh air is good for the lungs. Deep breath, Giuseppe slaps him on the back as he speaks.

Aroldaccio breathes in and catches the waft of Italian sauce from the kitchen. His feet, as those of a somnambulist, begin to move toward the smell.

Giuseppe turns him to the bar, *Aqua minerale for the champion!*

Marina puts out a selection of table waters, Aroldaccio has nothing against water but ... from somewhere deep down inside him comes a barely articulate moan, *Pizza.*

Pizza, dizza, drinka! Drink, amico mio, forget pizza on Friday 3 o'clock you can have ten pizzas all on top of one another. Giuseppe imitates an action of putting one pizza on top of another as he speaks.

Aroldaccio can already see them vividly before him. He puts his hands forward as if to grasp them. Giuseppe takes his arm as one might a sleepwalker's and leads him to a side table. They sit down.

All that food no good for you, heart attacks, Giuseppe can see from the big boy's eyes he's just not getting through. *We gotta talk, serious talking, understand?*

Aroldaccio stares.

Giuseppe shakes him, *Giuliana, Giuliana you know, Marina get Giuliana!*

She comes in with her daughter.

See Giuliana's leg, bad leg, understand?

Marina interrupts Giuseppe by kneeling down beside Aroldaccio and taking one of his massive biceps in both her hands, *Mia figlia, my daughter, my Giuliana, I beg you, for the Mother of God, help my daughter.*

She breaks into uncontrollable sobbing. Marina would have brought the house down in a Victorian melodrama. But her daughter does mean everything to her.

Giuseppe is telling him about how Giuliana was run down. *Quel figlio d'putt-, that son of a' just left her lying in the street.*

As Giuseppe speaks Aroldaccio sees the whole incident in his mind. The son of a' in a convertible driving off. He pictures himself chasing the automobile, running along the sidewalk … someone comes out of a shop carrying a tray of pies, they collide. A huge warm meat pie is lying on the sidewalk. He (the Aroldaccio of his own mind) bends down to pick it up.

Giuseppe is shaking his arm, *That son of a'!*

Aroldaccio jumps up knocking the table over, fists clenched, face flushed, *Where's the son of a', show me the son of a'!*

Giuseppe and Marina calm him down and get him seated. *Forget the son of a', it won't help Giuliana now. She needs operations. This man will pay for them.* Giuseppe motions to Macgreedy who steps forward bearing a serious expression which in him invariably implies calculation. He is afraid Aroldaccio won't take on the bet.

Giuseppe looks straight at the big guy, *All you gotta do is not eat, not eat for two days. Friday 3 o'clock you can eat as much as you want. Next week I'll organise an eating contest, pizzas. You against five guys, ten guys, we'll get you in the newspapers, the TV, we'll get you on Ed Sullivan's. Jus' say you'll do it.*

Marina on her knees again pleading with tear-stained eyes, *For Giuliana.*

The people in the café move a little closer, all telling him he can do it, willing him to go for it.

Even Macgreedy with a clenched fist, *Say yeah, go for it, big guy.*

Nothing was ever expected of Aroldaccio. Nobody ever really asked anything of him. Nobody ever really expected anything from him – except that he would eat. And that expectation he fulfilled with joyous over abundance.

Aroldaccio looks across at Giuliana and then down at her bad leg. *Yeah, yeah, okay I'll do it.*

Cheering breaks out.

Macgreedy puts his arms up for quiet, *We'll give the kid a break and ask Giuseppe not to serve food in the joint before eight o'clock this evening.*

This apparently benign gesture serves a double purpose. Firstly it allows Sir Giorgio to make a show of magnanimity. Macgreedy is not the kind of guy who is loved or expects to be loved. But it satisfies him when people respect him or when he can do something with the trappings of authority and generosity of a medieval lord.

Secondly and more importantly he doubts Aroldaccio will last half an hour when hot food is served to other customers.

Macgreedy reckons a breathing space will be needed for people to lay their bets. If the big guy can hold out a further hour or two then in the Latin quarter's group-generated exuberance he might be able to take in a thousand bucks or more.

Perhaps to give the proceedings a sense of ceremony the one who first proposed the wager quotes a couple of passages from Dante's *Inferno* in Italian. He then turns to Aroldaccio and, with an air of a parson conducting a wedding, speaks with a very English English accent, *Are you Aroldaccio prepared to take this upon yourself to fast for two days and two nights, that Giuliana may receive the treatment she needs, are you?*

Aroldaccio gulps as he answers in a dry whisper, *Yeah.*

Then I can tell you, my dear Aroldaccio, you will face an opponent greater than any you have yet faced. Greater than the Beast from New York State.

Aroldaccio sees again in memory that tattooed, hairy and vile sweating ex-sailor giving him a venomous squint before their steak-eating contest.

Greater than the Gorilla-Man from the Borneo Jungle.

Aroldaccio remembers the huge protruding lower jaw of the Gorilla-Man opening to take in bananas two or three at a time just as an ordinary person might pop in peanuts.

Yet both these opponents were carried out on stretchers.

Today Aroldaccio you will face – the speaker pauses.

In his imagination Aroldaccio sees himself facing a huge and shadowy presence at a contest.

Yourself!

In his mind's eye Aroldaccio looks across at his own double who smiles sardonically back at him.

He jumps to his feet (not in his mind) knocking over the table again, shouting and shaking his fist, *I'll eat him under the table!*

Calm, Calm, take it easy, Giuseppe's voice is trembling with Latin excitement, *Not eat, drink, drink him under the table, maybe.*

He manages to get Aroldaccio seated at the table just as Marina comes over with a large jug containing about two and a half pints of water. Aroldaccio grabs the jug and downs the water with one long swig.

Then burps.

The man, who originally proposed the bet, engages Giuseppe in a short but earnest exchange of words, writes something on a scrap of paper and hands it to Giuseppe before glancing back at Aroldaccio and calling out, *Buona fortuna!* as he leaves the café with a wave.

The Latin quarter buzzes in the next three or four hours. Nobody as yet is putting heat on Aroldaccio, the foodstuff with most calories being served in the joint is espresso. Three or four bottles of mineral water and a jug of tap water stand on the table in front of him. He gazes dazedly as people come in to place their bets and stare at him as though he were a rare animal in a cage.

Macgreedy was dead right about the group-generated ground-swell. By seven thirty there's close on two grand riding on the big guy. Giuseppe nips out and gets a promise of a hundred dollars from owners of five of the most successful eating houses.

$2500 dollars at odds of 2 to 1 that makes $5000 from Macgreedy if the wager is won, so now everything depends on the big guy, the one nobody has ever yet lost a bet on.

What people don't realise about Aroldaccio is that his imagination is as potent as his digestion. What ordinary people only experience in dreams or under the influence of hallucinogenic drugs is a natural part of his daily make-up. He becomes 'ordinary' only after ingesting a heavy meal. Then it's as though the vitality and vividness of his inner picturing is sucked into his digesting. With a full and distended stomach he can look out onto the world about him as you or I do.

Aroldaccio was never a night howler. At about the time children are being put to bed he is generally wending his way back to his one-bedroomed flat. Although you might not think it to look at him there is something cat-like about Aroldaccio. After a day spent eating he can sit for two, sometimes three hours in his broken armchair with his eyes half-closed just tasting the day's food right into his bowels, even into his blood stream.

His home has no and needs no TV, video, stereo, game console or computer. If his consciousness could give expression to itself as he sits in his chair, we would surely hear a purr, a loud and contented purring.

And like a cat (or a child) he can still sleep ten or twelve hours at a time.

Nobody ever told Aroldaccio that instead of holding down his fantasy by gnawing legs of roast pork and shovelling in potatoes ... that he might have been able to train his ability to make pictures in his mind. Maybe he could have created an imaginative literary landscape to rival Tolkien's Middle Earth, yet instead of opening the secret gate in his imagination he continually guts his picturing power with platefuls of greasy fries.

Then again nobody told many on a slippery slope toward psychotic conditions and a life on medicines that if at an early stage of their illness they had emulated Aroldaccio and gotten stuck into their victuals, done plenty and plenty of physical exercise, and trained the vividness of their inner picturing through the discipline of reading the world's great literature, instead of putting off the confrontation with their fantasy while sitting in front of a TV until that time of sleeplessness (or the sleeping pill) which awaits them later; they might never have needed to blight their lives with nerve medicine.

Then again nobody ever told millions of kids eager for a life for themselves as raw and gripping as the films they see (a rawness many buy with narcotics and their own destruction) that the same potency of experience awaits anyone who refrains from both drugs and Aroldaccio-like over indulgence and who seeks to take those paths in their imagination which lead West of the Moon, East of the Sun. (Do you know what Tolkien meant by "where many paths and errands meet"?)

Macgreedy and a pair of cohorts are at the far end of the café playing cards. Giuseppe and Aroldaccio are at a side table near the middle. Giuseppe's hope is water, to keep Aroldaccio satiated on liquid not solids. Whenever he moans Giuseppe tells him to drink. He's already downed a gallon and is experiencing abdominal pains. Not only his gut, his bladder is also suffering from excessive dilation. Yet as he stares around the café the ache of his overstretched urine reservoir seems far away.

His bladder suddenly remonstrates with a stab of violent pain. He groans, struggles to his feet but finds the pain makes it hard to walk upright. He puts his hands on the backs of chairs as he moves along. Macgreedy and his sidekicks jump up surrounding the big guy and Giuseppe.

He's supposed to stay here.

He's gonna relieve himself. You wanna watch him squirt?

They make way. Aroldaccio still bending goes toward relief. He is beginning to leak. Just before the door Macgreedy gets in front of him.

They'll check it out first.

The cohorts go in and leisurely search every inch of the lavatory, even smelling the liquid soap to make sure it hasn't been replaced by tomato sauce.

Aroldaccio has to turn sideways to get through the door. As he stands in position both of his enormous shoulders rub against the narrow walls. Desperation is bearable because relief is only an unzipping away. He reaches for the zip. Relief is coming. He fumbles with the zip. Relief bursts free from containment.

It slowly dawns on Aroldaccio that his trousers are the button-up type.

He comes back in dripping.

Marina rescues the situation. A blanket is wrapped around Aroldaccio's hind quarters and he gives up his pants to be washed.

It's eight thirty. Macgreedy and his cronies, having ordered all manner of culinary delicacies, are grumbling about sluggish service. Giuseppe is trying to stretch it out as long as possible before bringing food to the customers. But from the kitchen warm smells of Italian sauces drift in. Aroldaccio is alone at his table moaning softly like a lover.

Giuseppe is urgently whispering to Marina, *The one who got all this going said we should keep getting him to talk about his past life, his childhood.*

He goes over to the big boy and begins to ask him questions but can't seem to get through to him. Then he gives Aroldaccio's arm a violent shake, *What was the first thing you remember?*

The first thing I remember, er, he looks at Giuseppe as though suddenly aware of where he is, *Yeah, em, my third birthday party. Momma made two birthday cakes, one for me and one for my friends. And mine was the biggest! But-*

There is a pause.

Yeah, but what?

She wouldn't give it me.

What?

Aroldaccio seems far away again.

What? What wouldn't she give you?

Momma wouldn't give it to me.

What, a birthday present?

Momma wouldn't let me have it.

What? What didn't you get?

The nipple.

Breastfeeding had been a nutritional supplement for Aroldaccio until he was three years old. At a certain point in the birthday festivities he'd demanded it. And kept shouting after it and crying, *I want it, I want it!*

He jumped up and down in front of his mother trying to reach them.

It was a defining moment in Aroldaccio's life.

Macgreedy has moved closer. He was listening to the conversation and relishing Aroldaccio's present predicament. He pulls up a chair at Giuseppe's table and nudges Aroldaccio.

Are you a breast man or a leg man, big guy?

I've never been a Best Man, answers Aroldaccio innocently.

His mind flips back to the only wedding he'd attended as an adult. It was a big do with over a hundred guests, only one or two notches down from a society wedding. For Aroldaccio the ceremony had seemed interminable. Then they came to the reception hall and began to take photographs outside. He had other things on his mind and went into the foyer of the building. In a little alcove was a trolley with something on it that was draped over. He went to snoop. It was the wedding cake. He got behind the trolley, put his head under the cloth and began to amuse himself.

The photographers really took their time. Eventually everyone came in to the reception. Aroldaccio mingled with the others.

At the end of the meal, after most of the speeches, the big moment came, the trolley was wheeled in. Aroldaccio went into a cold sweat. The cake was unveiled.

It resembled a ruined Greek temple: a few fallen pillars on top of rubble, white icing pillars on top of crumbs – and plastic figures of a bride and groom with plastic smiles.

Aroldaccio's memories light up for him as quickly as a butterfly might open and close its wings while sipping nectar from a flower.

Giuseppe elbowing his arm brings his attention back to the café, *Non c'é cosa nostra, it's not our thing legs and* – Giuseppe makes a gesture. *It's not our thing, eh, big guy, non c'é Cosa Nostra!* emphasizing these last two words as he looks across at Macgreedy.

Aroldaccio isn't following at all (in fact he can still taste those mouthfuls of cake) but Macgreedy's face darkens, and he goes back to the table with his goons. Giuseppe knows all the gossip. Macgreedy was cuckolded by his first wife with a hit-man from Cosa Nostra.

I mean what do you do when your wife comes home with a Mafioso hit-man – except lie on the couch in the living room and bring them breakfast in bed as ordered.

This experience redefined Macgreedy's life.

The next one and a half hours are nightmarish for Aroldaccio. Food: pasta of all varieties, pizza ... pass before him. People are eating, eating all around but there's not a single spaghetti strand for him. The sidekicks are making a show of sucking and nibbling their pasta while seeking to catch Aroldaccio's eye. Giuseppe and Marina take it in turns to pump him about his biography. But no matter what they ask, he always brings his memories around to food and then his attention goes out to the people eating in the café.

Once when he is alone, Macgreedy comes up and puts $20 down on his table, *Anything you want, big boy, just order. George Macgreedy will pay.*

Aroldaccio picks up the money and wonders if it would buy a bathtub full of spaghetti and sauce. He imagines himself in a bath of lukewarm spaghetti sucking strands ten at a time.

Giuseppe comes to the rescue, *No bribery!* and takes the money out of the big guy's hands and shoves it in Macgreedy's breast pocket. He shakes the big guy, *Look, omaccio, here comes Marina with something special for you. Not still water, not fizzy carbonated water but naturally sparkling water. All the bubbles come into the water in underground streams and caves. Can you see those big dark caverns?*

It's no problem at all for Aroldaccio to picture caves and underground streams and lakes. And in lakes there are fishes ... fish roasting on a spit over a log fire beside an underground lake.

Mm, fish! licking his lips.

Time is moving on but there's a rising desperation on Aroldaccio's face. Marina's beginning to panic. Quite how the idea came into Giuseppe's mind is uncertain but he breaks into song.

When young he'd fancied himself as an operatic tenor like Caruso. Now he has the gruff baritone of a Sardinian bandit not the clear tones of a Venetian gondolier. But he has always loved Italian operas and operettas ... and he is singing Puccini.

The best adjective to describe his performance is probably 'loud'. But the main objective is achieved, to gain attention. Even Aroldaccio looks over at him. He gets a few cheers and claps. The sidekicks jeer. Giuseppe blows them kisses. Then he grabs hold of Marina, *Ladies and Gentlemen, Italian love songs from Marina!* He whispers in her ear, *For Giuliana,* and pushes her forward.

She too catches the moment. And begins a popular Italian song. She takes Aroldaccio's hand and looks at him with dark-eyed Latin longing. Una bellissima voce, her voice is just great. Not even the goons jeer. Aroldaccio claps.

Giuseppe calls for an encore ... and time is moving on.

Ten o'clock Giuseppe closes the kitchen and stands ready to pounce on the plates of anybody who breaks off eating. Soon the food and its smells are gone ... and the worst crisis over. The tables are shoved back against the walls and mattresses carried in. The one for Aroldaccio is big and put smack in the middle of the dining area. The other mattresses are set as far away from his as possible.

By around midnight the lights are lowered. Seven people remain: Giuseppe and Macgreedy at the bar with drinks; the others, all stretched out on mattresses, are a couple of Latins designated to check on the bet, the two Macgreedy sidekicks and the big boy himself.

Macgreedy goes to take a last look at Aroldaccio who is staring up at the ceiling and whimpering. A sudden urge rises up in Sir Giorgio to walk over him and to stamp on the guts of the swelled-up shape below him.

Urges in Macgreedy rarely break into direct action. This urge now restrained comes to expression as a smile of triumph. To his mind there is no way the inflated hulk on the floor can last out tomorrow, probably not even the night. So his mood is cheery as he leaves and walks jauntily back the few blocks to his apartment.

For more than an hour Aroldaccio lies there, too weak too move, too weak to open the bottle of table water beside him. He lets out long wailing tones which fade into sighs and then rise again in high-pitched murmurs and moans. None of the others can get to sleep.

Eventually this wailing gives way to heavy groans and then quite suddenly Aroldaccio's motor-mower snores splutter into the room.

And continue. And continue.

None of the others get much sleep at all.

Aroldaccio dreams he's in a cellar or prison cell. At the top of one wall and on street level is a small opening with bars. From outside as though from far away come sounds of children playing. He stands on tiptoes and peers through the bars. People are selling all kinds of edibles. It seems like a market place. He pushes his arm through the bars and begs for food. No one takes any notice. Then a child drops some nuts as she runs by. He tries to grab a nut but can't seem to pick it up.

You can't.

The voice from behind him is female.

He turns to see a young woman sitting in the cell. In front of her is a small low table.

You can't. You haven't got a body.

Of course I've got a body. I am a body!

Aroldaccio tries to prove his assertion by pounding on his chest like a gorilla.

No sound comes.

No body, she says shaking her head.

But I'm hungry.

How can you eat without a body?

Aroldaccio notices a glass of water and a crust of bread on the table. The water doesn't hold much interest for him, but the bread!

Is it your bread?

She gestures for him to take it. He tries to pick it up. Not even with two hands can he get it off the table. He gets on his knees, gives the woman an embarrassed smile, and tries to bite it with his mouth like a dog.but he can't get his teeth into it.

She shakes her head sadly, *You haven't got a body.*

Aroldaccio suddenly feels he's dreaming, that he's in a dream. He decides to try to sleep away his dream and curls up on the floor of the cell.

(Have you ever tried to go to sleep in a dream?)

Aroldaccio goes to sleep in this dream … and wakes in another. Where he is a child, much reduced in bulk, playing with other children …

The night also awaits Macgreedy.

Walking home on an air of pride, he is proud to be the one to squeeze green from Latin pockets. Macgreedy never really considered himself a Latin. He always felt a little apart from them, superior in some sense, and was happiest when he could use Latins to run errands or egg them into taking losing bets. Yet he spent all his time in the Latin milieu. Their company was familiar and congenial. His wives were all from Latin American families. And though in some vague way he thought of himself as a Scot, he knew no Scots and only a very few Anglo-Saxon Americans on any meaningful level.

As a boy he used to picture himself with super powers. Kid Suction Hands: to point his hand at someone's purse and imagine all their money sucked into his palm. Now stepping lightly along the sidewalk he pretends to pretended people on the street that he's suck-zapping their wallets.

He falls asleep chuckling but soon begins to dream ... He is counting, counting out greens in wads of ten. He seems to be in a cool and dimly lit cellar. A table is in front of him. Whenever he puts a pile of money on the table a hand appears from out of nowhere to steal it away. Until he thinks out a system: Whenever he has a wad of ten he puts it under his armpit.

He is counting and counting. When he can get no more under his armpits he puts wads behind his knees, then between his ankles, between his thighs. When there is no place left between his legs he puts them under his chin. Then in his mouth.

There is still more money to count so he hits on the ingenious scheme to put the next wad on the table and to quickly put his forehead down on it.

He has now about half a dozen wads of money under his brow, he is pressing his arms tightly into his body, his legs together, his chin down – and trying not to get the wads in his mouth too wet.

And still he is counting.

Rustling sounds, a breeze fresh as from a woodland, squinting over at the doorway Macgreedy sees a tall female figure surrounded by light. She is sterner than the maid in Aroldaccio's prison cell, more like a Prussian Mädchen with a long dress from the eighteenth century, only there is nothing 'chen' or petite about her.

He thinks he hears her say something like a guttural *Raus*. She moves closer. He can't move for fear of losing his wads of money. She puts her face near to his and in soft song-like tones says, *Wir müssen rein machen*. Then standing tall again she puts it in loud and happy-go-lucky American, *We'll have to clean you out, hon!*

She glides over to a corner. Macgreedy sees there a vacuum cleaner, an industrial type bigger than a washing machine. It begins to whirr.

She marches over pointing the sucker end at him. The money under his brow disappears down the sucker and his forehead bangs down on the hard cold table. She points it at his ankles, his knees, his armpits … every dollar is vacuumed away.

Macgreedy is now the fierce Scot standing upright his head about the same height as her chest, clutching in his left hand a fistful of dollars, biting on a couple of wads between his teeth and growling.

She points it at his mouth, the wads of money and his false teeth shoot into the sucker. She points it at his left arm, the suction drags him forward, his hand disappears down the sucker. With rage and strain he pulls out his arm ... only there is nothing below the elbow. His left arm is a stump.

Not finished, hon', not finished with you yet!

His shirt, trousers, shoes, all go the same way down the sucker. He is rooted there in his underpants and socks, and he can't seems to move a muscle. She brings the sucker down to his shin. He cries out in desperate pain as the hair on his legs feels as if it's being ripped from his skin.

She smiles sweetly at him and, as the sucker end draws nearer his crotch, she whispers, *Checkmate!*

... all becomes blackness and excruciation.

Lying in bed in the early morning Macgreedy's mood is grim and dark. From the moment of waking he knew he'd been trapped, caught in a no-win situation.

Win and he'd always be seen as the one who took money away from Giuliana. They might go on calling him Sir Giorgio but the respect will be gone. He knows the Latins. They'd probably start whispering about Cosa Nostra and making gestures of cuckold horns behind his back.

Lose and a part of one of his Swiss bank accounts will disappear. Yet maybe even more than the money is the thought of losing. The thought that he who always places the certain bet – will have been made to look dumb by a pumped-up gump like Aroldaccio and outsmarted by Giuseppe and Marina.

As he lies there he realises there is an escape route; he can call a truce: $2500 of their bets and $2500 of his own money to pay for Giuliana's opps. It'll cost him but he'll retain his respect among them, even enhance it by this show of magnanimity. Yes perhaps but in his own mind he'll know he's been forced into a corner and feel cheated.

The face of his favourite literary character comes up before him. He sees so clearly the long pock-marked nose, the rounded back, the goatee beard, the squinting features: Shylock. Macgreedy is back in his youth, in his school days when they read *The Merchant of Venice.*

He'd always been able to see Shylock. The other characters in the play were vague proud pretty-boys but Shylock for him was real.

There in its closing scenes when Portia disguised as a lawyer is offering him a great return on his loan to Antonio, Macgreedy had been on tenderhooks unsure of whether he hoped his hero would take the money or not.

Shylock about to take his triumph with the knife blade before the bare chest of his enemy – for Macgreedy this was the most potent image in literature.

Then Portia checkmated his hero: Flesh but not a drop of blood. Everything went wrong. The pretty-boys took the lot. Macgreedy was sure of one thing: If he'd been checkmated as Shylock, he'd have taken the flesh, he'd have used the knife.

This had been a defining moment in Macgreedy's growing up.

And yet when his first wife came back with the Mafioso, he put on an apron in the kitchen and quietly made them breakfast.

Shylock saved Macgreedy, saved him from possible involvement with Far Right movements. Their rallying call of a 'superior' race which brings to heel 'inferior' races, blacks, immigrants, commies, people on Medicare or social security, civil-rights campaigners, women interested in ecology and suchlike folk who are blamed for all ills – might have proved seductive to the young Macgreedy, had it not been for the fact that Jews were generally classified as being in this 'lesser' category. Not that he really knew any Jews but because of Shylock and their legendary business shrewdness, they were heroes in his eyes. If ever this third wife of his dies (or comes back with an Italian) his fourth will be Jewish no matter if she looks like the rear of a tractor.

His wife comes into the bedroom with a tray of coffee and pancakes. Macgreedy is set to go on as he started, straight for the naked victory.

Aroldaccio wakes refreshed, without a pillow, a fist or even anything imagined in his mouth. He raises himself on an elbow. Marina and Giuliana are smiling down at him.

I wanna play football.

The Latins at the bar begin to cheer. Giuseppe has left the tables more or less how they were so Aroldaccio wouldn't be disturbed. The two mutts are sat at a corner table, bleary-eyed through lack of sleep and each with a double espresso. Macgreedy has just arrived. He signals to his mutts, *The big guy wants to play football*. Then turning to Giuseppe, *Hasn't one of your teenagers got a football?* Macgreedy reckons the more motion Aroldaccio gets the hungrier he'll become.

The big guy and the goons toss the football to each other in the free space in the middle of the café.

That a boy! Go for it!

Giuseppe's words remind him of his school football coach. At school Aroldaccio was super at football (the American kind). He was nicknamed the Running Blob.

When he got the ball in his hands he just ran (and he could run mighty quick then). He just stampeded for the line. Anybody in his way got trampled. In training the other kids used to make it an art to look as though they were tackling him while actually trying to get out of his path. At fourteen he was over six foot and huge of frame.

He could probably have made it as a professional but gave up after little more than half a semester at college. Training sessions got in the way of more serious pursuits. They often had to be on the field for more than an hour with no breaks to eat. He used to hide snacks under his gear. Once he smuggled a large meat pie out onto the pitch. He was guzzling it when the quarterback threw him the ball. Rather than let go of the meat pie he tried to catch the ball with one hand, dropped it and was blown out by the college coach, dismissed from training and suspended. So he went back home and just kind of wallowed in food. He never returned to college. And underwent, you could say, metamorphosis from the Running to the Bloated Blob.

When Giuseppe said, "Go for it!" Aroldaccio felt himself as a strapping fifteen-year old running for the line. His sudden transformation took the sidekicks totally off guard. They knew nothing about trying to make a pretence of tackling while really getting out of the way – and so were caught in the stampede.

After running them over Aroldaccio ran right into the wall at the far end and sort of bounced back, falling on top of them as they lay groaning on the floor.

Marina and Giuseppe did a great job of getting the big guy to talk about his teenage love of sport, and kept the conversation away from you know what. But as midday neared and people were ordering lunches the crisis erupted.

In the orgy of eating, with Macgreedy and his sidekicks eyeing the big guy as they take grizzly bites of pizza, it is impossible for Giuseppe to get through to him. Aroldaccio whines. The sound is something like hearing a dog in the distance as it howls at the moon.

Giuseppe gives up and goes over to Marina.

He'll never make it. What do you do with kids, little kids, bambini, who always want to eat?

Marina brushes her hair back, it looks as if tears are about to come to her eyes. She walks away then stops. Her expression changes, brightens, she lets out an Italian shriek of excitement, *Bambini! Big enough for Aroldaccio! Giuliana said it was big enough for Aroldaccio! Be back in a sec.*

She leaves. After about ten minutes she returns with a paper bag.

Aroldaccio has his head in his hands. Giuseppe is standing resignedly over him. Marina goes straight to their table. *Aroldaccio*, she sings more than speaks, *Close your eyes and open your mouth.*

He does as he's told. He generally does as he's told. Marina takes out of the paper bag a pacifier (what the English call a dummy) of giant proportions. The plastic disk is as big as a saucer, the ring big enough for a bull and the rubber teat as large as a small slim pear. She pops it in.

Straight away as if by instinct he begins to suck. Aroldaccio gazes around the café. Macgreedy toasts him with a forkful of fettuccine. Aroldaccio sucks harder. A woman at the opposite table is holding a spoonful of ice cream absent mindedly near her lips. He sucks on his comforter even harder, his cheeks all on the go, his neck reddening.

The pacifier was a display model on show in the window of a baby shop. Somehow Marina managed to entice them to loan it to her.

Fairytales! The one who started all this, said we might tell the big guy fairytales, Giuseppe snaps his fingers as he speaks and rushes off upstairs to find any old children's books. He comes back with a battered copy of fairytales from around the world or a similar sounding title.

Marina sits beside Aroldaccio and begins to read up for him. He pictures Jack climbing up the beanstalk. When the giant's voice resounds, "Fe, fi, fo, fum ..." the café, even the food becomes irrelevant. When Jack steals the goose that lays the golden eggs, he gapes so much that the dummy drops out of his mouth.

Time moves on – quickly for Aroldaccio as he lives in the stories. three o'clock, five o'clock, six o'clock ... whenever Marina stops reading and he catches sight of food he takes recourse to furious dummy sucking.

Giuseppe and Marina start to hope. Macgreedy for the first time begins to doubt. Aroldaccio is beyond doubt and hope, for him the experiences are too raw.

Giuliana started to laugh uncontrollably at the sight of Aroldaccio with his giant pacifier when she came to the café after school. She was quickly ushered into the kitchen by her mother. Whenever she popped her head round the kitchen door she got the giggles.

Then it struck her he was lacking something.

Momma, can't you find Aroldaccio something to play with, a big rattle or something?

Giuseppe overheard. Sometime later he remembered the African shaking sticks, at least that's what his kids used to call them. Simple instruments made from a stick with a dried pod as big as a fist attached. Inside the pod are dried peas or beans which rattle when you move it. He fetched a pair of shaking sticks and gave them to the big guy so Aroldaccio would be able to shake as well as suck if no one happened to be reading a story to him.

Around half past six an elderly and overly upper-class British couple on holiday enter the café.

Oh, Gerald I do just adore this ethnic atmosphere. Do order something very, mm, very Italian.

They are shown to a table nearly opposite Aroldaccio's. He isn't there, he's relieving himself. The sidekicks are waiting outside the lavatory door. One of them is peeping through the keyhole and holding his nose.

The English couple are sipping soup with upper-class ostentation when Aroldaccio complete with pacifier returns. He seats himself and begins to suck with gusto as he sees them eating.

Er, Gerald, I say, hasn't that man over there a dummy in his mouth?

Aroldaccio picks up his shaking sticks and starts to shake them.

I think that's what they call a go-go dancer, my dear.

The English Lady is not convinced. She calls over Marina, *I say, is he dangerous?*

Em, fancy dress, sort of practising fancy dress.

You see my dear, just as I told you, he is going to a masquerade as a go-go dancer.

Macgreedy and his cronies are at the adjacent table to Aroldaccio and nearer to the bar. Pasta with steaming cheese sauce is being served to them.

Macgreedy has his back to the wall like Aroldaccio. The crony facing Macgreedy takes a forkful of spagetti and smirks at Aroldaccio while making fish-like nibbling motions with his mouth.

Aroldaccio responds with violent shark-like motions of his jaws as he works away on his dummy. Macgreedy holds up a forkful of pasta and winks at Aroldaccio.

The ring and plastic disk of the pacifier suddenly fall from Aroldaccio's mouth. He lurches up, knocks over his own table, tramples the goon sittting opposite Macgreedy and causes their table to tilt backwards. Macgreedy's plate slides towards him, falls off and deposits pasta with steaming sauce in his lap. Macgreedy is still holding up the forkful of pasta to his mouth.

It takes about two seconds for the burning heat of pasta and sauce to reach his private parts. He jumps up bellowing.

And is forced to cool his crotch with a jug of water. Meanwhile Aroldaccio storms toward the bar bent forward and holding his chest. He bit off the teat from the dummy and it stuck in his throat choking him. The emergency passes when he vomits the teat and the liquid contents of his stomach onto the floor.

Meanwhile the English gentleman lifts his glass of red wine, *Those go-go dancers do adore making a show of themselves! Do taste the wine, my dear, it's Orvietto 52.*

Aroldaccio was led quietly back to his table where he spent the rest of the evening being read to by Marina. The

English couple drank two bottles of Orvietto 52 and stayed until ten o'clock. Marina received a big tip from them.

The English gent takes her hand as they are about to leave, *Wonderful to hear fairytales again. Haven't heard any since the governess read to us over 60 years ago. Do you know 'The Princess and the Goblin'? Always wanted to be a miner like Curdie but ... but the Old Man would have none of it.*

He shakes his head a little.

Ahm! At this fairly loud injection from his wife, he lets go of Marina's hand.

With fond farewells the old couple leave.

The second evening is passing. Mattresses are brought in again. Macgreedy decides to sleep in the café. As do Marina and her daughter; Marina in the kitchen, Giuliana upstairs with Giuseppe's family.

About half an hour after midnight. The lights in the café are out. Everyone is lying down. Aroldaccio's snores remind Macgreedy of a pneumatic drill. He sees road workers digging a hole in the street; he climbs down into it, he is descending ... into dream ...

He's back in the cellar, it is gloomier than before but undoubtedly the place of yesterday's dream. He stands very still straining to keep alert in the dark.

That same rustling sound and rush of breeze – the Prussian maid is before him surrounded by light.

He involuntarily cups his hands over his private parts.

How yer feelin' today, honey? She holds out her hand to him, *Come on hon', I'll take you upstairs.*

She looks more familiar than in yesterday's dream, safely familiar with a compassionate clearness in her eyes. Macgreedy gives an audible sigh of relief.

Over her left arm is draped a coat, light grey in colour, and resembling a pre-war great coat. She puts it on him. And takes his hand.

Outside the door is a winding stone stairway. Up they walk, up and up and up. Before them is a solid oak door. The Prussian maid opens it and invites him with a gesture to enter. It is a large circular dome-shaped space full of people all standing quietly.

As Macgreedy walks in he recognises a woman who greets him warmly. As they exchange a few words he finds he can remember everything the two of them ever did together; the good moments, the cross words ... then he notices an old school chum. The moment Macgreedy takes his eye away from her she stands still as a statue. But his school friend comes to life.

The Prussian maid guides him firmly through this gathering of people. Each one is known to Macgreedy, some from just a single conversation on a bus. Near the centre of the room is a four-poster bed. He draws aside a curtain. In the bed are his Colombian first wife and the hit-man sitting quietly. As Macgreedy looks at him the man from Cosa Nostra comes to life, *Hey Mac, you know that breakfast of pancakes you made me, best I ever ate.*

His Prussian guide pulls him gently away. The curtain closes behind him.

They reach the far side of the domed hall. Before them is an arched door above which are symbols.

Shall we go on? Or would you prefer, she points behind him, *Prefer to go back down?*

He turns around and sees a round opening in the floor with a spiral stairway leading down.

It's your choice.

My choice, my choice ...

Macgreedy's consciousness begins to awaken. He can vaguely hear Aroldaccio's noises which remind him of a dreaming lion. Macgreedy rolls over ... into a deeper sleep.

The night has also been waiting for Aroldaccio.

In his dream he is younger, not yet in his teens. Most of his adult bulk is gone. His walk is lighter. Alone in a dining room. The table decked with food for a party. He nibbles some popcorn, it's like paper in his mouth, the peanuts taste as though they're a decade old. He spits them out. Nothing tastes as it should.

He goes into another room. A large imposing table with hot roasts and steaming vegetables. He forks a potato and bites – powdery. Peas – hard as if frozen for a century. He breaks off a leg of chicken and tries to chew – rubbery. He takes a spoonful of gravy – yuk! And spits it all over the white table cloth and silver cutlery.

Then he runs into another room which is also full of food but all the wrong colours: turquoise cakes, purple sausages, pink popcorn, royal blue fizzy drinks. He doesn't stop but races out of the main doors into the sunshine.

Skipping, jumping, running ... he runs and runs ... suburban streets become city boulevards. His pace slows. He has become bigger and older. His bulk weighs him down. He slumps tired and panting on stone steps.

On his neck is a thick and studded dog-collar. He tries to heave it off. An iron chain attached to it is held by someone in uniform who tugs Aroldaccio up and leads him away further along the street. He puts up no fight against being led.

He finds himself in a cellar, that same cellar. The dog collar and chain are gone, he is alone. Outside the bars of his window come sounds of children shouting in the sunshine. People are pushing carts full of goods to eat. The waft of hot pies. He puts a hand through the bars and clutches after food but grasps only the air and sadly draws his arm back. And senses he is no longer by himself.

At the table behind him sits his maid sadly shaking her head, *You've got no body – how can you eat without a body?*

Aroldaccio looks down at himself, he seems to be fading. *I'm so hungry*, he mumbles.

The maid rises, goes to the door then turning back looks at him intently, *I shall ask*, she whispers and leaves.

As in yesterday's dream, bread is lying on the table. He makes a half-hearted attempt to pick it up but his fingers go through it. He kneels and waits.

Long he waits.

At last the door opens noiselessly. She beckons him. He struggles to his feet and goes after her. On reaching the door he turns back to look one last time at his cell. Kneeling on the floor is a faded figure exactly like himself.

Come quickly! her voice is urgent.

He walks behind her. Soon though she is far ahead of him as she lightly treads along a gloomy corridor. The only light is that which shimmers around her. He follows her through many passages. Always she is ahead of him, always he fears to lose her and be left alone in these dark dank tunnels.

She is gone. Aroldaccio cries out to her. His voice echoes, echoes into stillness. He stands in darkness afraid, afraid even to be afraid. Then he hears her call faintly from far ahead. He moves cautiously in the direction from which her voice came.

A fresh flower-filled draught of air in the gloom and Aroldaccio can see her shining figure framed by the end of a passageway. He begins to run.

Outside in a garden as on a warm and fragrant summer evening. She points upwards to the starlit sky. The stars seem closer, much closer. Even small stars are as bright as Jupiter on a clear night. The larger stars throb and shine. For a moment Aroldaccio wonders whether he could touch them if he jumped. He sees no moon.

She points to a corner of the garden where there is an opening in the rock. Side by side they walk toward it. He has to bow to enter. The grotto is spacious. On a stone table or altar is a goblet. In the light around her he sees the cup is of beaten gold with a base silver.

Kneel.

He obeys. She takes the chalice and shows him what it contains: Glowing red roses, half a dozen or more. She takes one and puts it in his open mouth.

It tastes as flowers smell, giving way to the flavour of freshly plucked berries with a wheat or nutty after taste on his tongue. Aroldaccio can taste it in his stomach astringent, hop-like. His inside glows.

Sleep Aroldo, dream the stars.

He sinks down and curls himself around his belly. The glow, the warm yet strangely bitter glow fills him.

He dreams many dreams. And always the rose warmth sustains him.

Before dawn he wakes. Emptiness inside him. The dream's fiery sustenance pervades him no more. An icy chill gnaws from his extremities to his innards. Aroldaccio is certain he is about to die.

He calls out in a dry choke and then again in a loud voice, *I am dying.*

Macgreedy is the first to his bed. He looks down at Aroldaccio's bloated form with mingled pity and disgust. Marina rushes in from the kitchen. Giuseppe tramps down the stairs in his dressing gown.

Please, the Last Rites! Let me have the Sacraments before I die, and after a pause, *So I can get to see the stars.*

Rapid-fire Italian from three or four at once.

He can't take the Sacraments. It would break the conditions of the bet. Unless, Giuseppe glances over to Macgreedy, *Unless Sir Giorgio agrees to it.*

Macgreedy speculates as he looks down at Aroldaccio, *Sure, let him take it.*

You'll put it on paper?

Sure.

But Macgreedy is unsure if he's agreeing out of compassion or because he reckons that once the big guy's digestive juices get on the go there'll be no stopping them. Maybe a bit of both.

Marina says the church on the next street has an early morning service. She grabs a coat and leaves.

Giuseppe and Macgreedy chat in the semi-darkness over an espresso. Aroldaccio groans in his bed.

About half an hour later Marina returns with a priest of about sixty years of age.

Okay, where's the dying one?

Giuseppe points. The priest kneels beside Aroldaccio and whispers.

Macgreedy interrupts, *Say, hasn't he got to be near death's door to be eligible for Last Rites?'*

Is this the guy who's fasting for Giuliana?

Marina nods.

Then maybe some part of him is dying. I'll take responsibility with – the priest makes a gesture heavenwards.

In the half light Aroldaccio thinks he sees a rose on the wafer. It dissolves on his tongue, the taste wholesome and as in the dream a warmth fills him from inside.

The priest ruffles his hair, *Sleep now. And maybe wherever you awake, it will be different.*

Aroldaccio curls up around the glow in his belly – and purrs, or at least his noises could almost be construed as a contented purring.

He sleeps and sleeps. Right through the morning he lies on the mattress in the centre of the café, unwilling to move or open his eyes; slumber is near, café noises far away – and inside is a glow he hopes will never leave him.

Latins file in to grab a quick espresso (Giuseppe has shrewdly halved their price) and to take a look at Aroldaccio.

Like a procession paying their last respects to a corpse, Macgreedy shakes his head as he speaks but there is a glint of fun in his eye.

You know, I figured you'd be in a black mood and scheming if it ever got this far.

Well Giuseppe, it's like this, maybe the money is better spent getting Giuliana right than stuck in some bank account. How much longer have I got – five, ten, fifteen years? I've no kids and how many friends? Of course there won't be much left after paying out.

You'd need a nose job if your name was Pinocchio.
They look at each other and burst out laughing.
When did I last laugh, Giuseppe, really laugh? He sips on the espresso before continuing, *With the bit, the little tiny bit, that's left over maybe I'll take a trip to Europe. Bonny Scotland: the Bens and the glens! Germany perhaps, I've always had a hankering to see how the Prussians live. And Venice!*

He pictures Shylock in a Jewish hat warily moving along a narrow Venetian street.

Aroldaccio pushes himself up on one arm. The Latins cheer him. Giuliana is sitting at their table with a pile of fairytale books, cries out, *Momma!*

Marina helps the big boy up and sits him beside her daughter.

A new tale?
No, the same as yesterday, Jack and the Beanstalk.

He insists on hearing it there times in a row. Seeing the story in his imagination, oblivious to surroundings, eyes half-closed, mouth half-open.

It's twenty to three. Marina has taken over from her daughter and is reading him stories. Macgreedy orders a drink. He lifts his glass, in his mind's eye he sees Shylock with a dagger, raising it as though to plunge the knife into something ... then he casts it away with all his strength into a Venetian canal. Shylock looks pointedly at Macgreedy.

Though he has often pictured Shylock, never until now has Shylock looked back at him. A hint of a smile under the Venetian's bushy eyebrows as if to say, "Well, now you know".

This last picture or vision of Shakespeare's Jewish moneylender is only there for a moment. But it leaves Macgreedy with a peace he savours for awhile.

Five to three, he stands up, raises his glass, *Friends, a toast to Giuliana's knight!*

Drinks on the house! shouts Giuseppe.

The big guy is still way off in fairytale adventures.

Macgreedy gets everybody's attention, *I'll let you into a little secret; even if Aroldaccio had failed the test I would still have paid for Giuliana.*

Latin exclamations and not a few jeers.

Yeah, it's true I would still have paid. (Who knows maybe he would have.) *But if I'm paying five grand, we're gonna get her the best, the very best!*

Giuseppe steps forward and takes out a piece of paper from his pocket. *That guy, the one who started all this off, gave me a name and address of a top surgeon in the next state. He said if we win we should take this guy.*

Monday, Giuseppe, you and me, Marina and Giuliana will all drive up and get it arranged. Macgreedy turns toward the big fellow and raises his glass, *To Aroldaccio!*

All that remains is for Giuliana's knight to break his fast. Everyone crowds round his table. Marina takes the order: *Starters?*

No Starters.

No starters! Marina raises an eyebrow, *Main course?*

Minastromi.

Minestrone and what?

No what, just minastromi.

Bread?

No bread.

Dessert?

Maybe.
Marina begins to reel off the names of desserts.
Pizza.
For dessert?
Yes pizza, Aroldaccio begins to use both his hands as he speaks, *Ten pizzas all piled one on top of the other.*

8. Adopting

One of the clearest memories I have of those stories was that ending where Aroldaccio requests ten pizzas all on top of one another. Everyone laughed. Sister Anna closed the book and we started to leave. Maria was chirpy too then she stopped and frowned. And she wasn't by me any more but going up to our nun.

Sister Anna went down on one knee as she always did if you came to ask her about something troubling you.

Please Sister Anna, will Aroldaccio just go back to being a glutton again? And what about his angel?

Sister Anna looked thoughtfully out of the window before answering. Maybe she didn't know herself what the continuation was or even if the story was to go on further.

Mm, don't you think Marina and Giuliana might adopt him?

That was enough for my sister she skipped over to me and began bubbling about how Marina and her daughter would get the 'Big One' cured of guzzling. Soon she was making up a story about this and I joined in. We thought up many a story together about the big guy. Funny how kids can worry over a character in a story. Is Aroldaccio real or just imagined? And what about the Dons: Quixote and Juan or Giovanni as Mozart and the Italians call him? Luckily such existential trickies don't belong to childhood. Aroldaccio was real enough for me and for my sister then.

We were nearly home when she asked me an odd sort of question, *Would you like to adopt kids, Ray?*

What do you mean adopt kids, I am a kid!

9. Premonitions

On Sunday mornings following the end of an angel story Sister Anna used to arrive with a few books. She'd ask us if we wanted to hear a legend about such and such a saint or prophet, presenting us with two or three choices. We'd listen politely as we sat dangling our legs on the chairs in the church hall. When she came to, *Well children, what would you like to hear?*

We'd all shoot back, *Angel stories! We want angel stories, angel stories, angel stories!*

Almost as soon as I woke up on those Sunday mornings I'd think: Sunday – angel stories! And just bounce up out of bed.

One Sunday at the end of the May we finished a story and contrary to usual practice, she just asked if we'd like another angel tale next week. I don't need to tell you our response.

Next Sunday came and alongside our Sister Anna another sister appeared. Taller, thinner and perhaps younger, this other nun wore glasses all the time and not just to read. Her lips narrow and taut, she never smiled. She looked directly at you but not to meet your gaze openly. Slightly screwing up her eyes she'd shoot her own sight into you. She didn't bend down to you, didn't go on one knee to listen as Sister Anna did. She'd bend over you, so it felt as if she were pressing herself into you – and you sort of wanted to fend her off with your hand.

'Coming-into-you eyes' was how Maria described them. Later we spoke of them as trespassing eyes.

Most kids referred to her (when she wasn't there!) as Sister Mousetrap – for reasons you'll hear about later. This probably makes her sound a lot more endearing than she actually was. I can't remember her name but I'm pretty sure it began with an 'M'.

When I try to come up with names for her I get things such as: Morbiditina, Murdara, Mesmerola, Misanthropa.

It's not easy to imagine her with a name like other people though. A code would have been more appropriate. Come to think of it, somebody said she arrived June Sixth and designated her M66.

M66 sounds like a section in the British Secret Service. If ever an 'agency' decides to assassinate the pope she'd make the ideal Manchurian candidate, the perfect Papal terminator.

Pervaded by Sister Anna's human warmth none of us quite realised that first time what an M66 session might entail. Except maybe one.

Maria didn't even try to sleep in her own bed that evening. As soon as mother went downstairs she sneaked into my room, crept under the bed clothes and held onto me most of the night.

It was about the only time I ever knew her wet the bed. My sister, not only did she daydream about angels she was blessed with a prophetic bladder!

Mother had never been keen on us sleeping together so I made up a feeble excuse (equivocation I think the Jesuits call it) about us having had too much to drink before going to bed. And as a reward every evening for half the Summer I was made to go and squirt in the garden before being allowed off to bed.

A brother and sister appeared in the new angel story. The boy was a couple of years older and envious of everything about his sister. If they ate cake he always thought her piece was biggest. If she got praised, he'd be resentful as hell. His biggest kicks came from being spiteful to her whenever their parents weren't around.

His angel endlessly sought to get him to see his sister as a playmate instead of a competitor, all to no avail. Faint whispers of conscience jammed in his earwax. The poor angel spent the nights enfolded in her wings shivering in the shadows beside the boy's bed.

It left me with a weird sensation. Maybe I hadn't always given Maria the biggest cake but I was real glad just to have her around, rarely envious and could hardly ever remember being purposely spiteful to her.

This tale invoked a shadow picture of anti-fraternal feuding, a counter-image of our play together. Of course then I didn't know terms like counter-image but it all made me creepy right down the backbone.

Me and Maria were sparrows frittering away on a sunny afternoon; that pair wasps caught in a spider's snare, each trying to jab poison in the other's butt.

It's one thing hearing about Cain and Abel but you don't expect to meet them in the snack bar. Whereas the kid in this story could having been sitting in the next desk at school.

Everything fell flat, none of us laughed. There were no sniffles or runny eyes. Even the chocolate cake in the story tasted stale. Definitely an off-day for Sister Anna. Maybe she was not with it because her mother was dying.

Or was it because M66 was already beginning to spin her webs?

She sat a little apart from Sister Anna and watched us. We weren't much aware of her, not consciously anyway. At one point though I distinctly remember shuddering and involuntarily glancing over to her narrowed lids as her sight scanned through me.

Walking back without words along the path through the trees, me kicking the odd stone, Maria with a bowed head alongside me in her red cotton dress and sandals. All at once she grabbed my hand in both of hers, *Why was her brother so envious?*

I don't know.
Why didn't his sister buy him a chocolate bar?
I don't know.
Me looking down at her, she up at me.
Do brothers and sisters really feel like that, Ray?
I don't know, I just don't know.

She dropped her head again but kept one hand tightly gripping mine as we shuffled further along the path. Then I sighed and stopped, clenching my teeth I lifted my hand with hers still attached up to my chest, *But you can be sure as peanut butter's made from peanuts, Maria, I ain't gonna spite you.*

Two in misery is less than one. (Qualitative mathematics: $-1 + (-1) = -½$ if there's a genuine plus between.).

Strange how on a day when something's gonna happen you wake up and know it. I mean, not know it exactly but some part of you knows it. The following Sunday none of us knew Sister Anna had already left to be beside her dying mother. None of us knew her replacement was at hand ... but we knew it, we knew it somewhere inside us.

First Maria came clattering down the stairs and clouted her knee. Then I burnt my hand. Mother stayed home. We two walked through the woods, slowly because her knee was swelling, and held hands most of the way.

And I suppose if we could have risen up, not only in space but also in time, to look down at ourselves (two children walking hand in hand through the trees) and been able to see what we were heading toward ... then maybe we'd have swapped places with Hansel and Grettel.

... to be continued.

10. Hiding

About the only attempts my sister ever made to conceal anything were when she tried to hide her feelings if something hurt her.

She could be listening to a tale about a dog waiting for its deceased owner. Tears wouldn't so much be welling as flowing in streams down her cheeks. Yet she'd hardly notice for inwardly she'd be seeing the dog forlornly whining at the railway station for the master who would never return.

But if she bruised her elbow or fell awkwardly she'd bite her lip and dig in to keep her eyes from watering or turn away and bottle up the pain. She was pretty good at deflecting or even not noticing snide remarks. But if some comment did stab her, she'd react similarly and a short but intense trial would ensue to reign herself in and quell any gush of emotion from forming on her features.

I couldn't stand hurting her. Close though as we two were, there was no chance of always avoiding it, but it'd carve me up if I did, leave me feeling real bad.

With us being so natural together, with most every passing emotion shining unhampered through her then almost without trying, I evolved a sensitivity to discern when anything began to get to her. I learnt how to tease her for hours and yet realise immediately when a limit was being approached which if overstepped would make her sore.

It had been a good school growing up with my sister for developing the tact of knowing when and how one's self impinges on another. As for Maria she didn't seem to need to learn this tact, she was born with it.

If I was born with anything it was a sense for knowing when she needed to be by herself. Something Maria had to learn.

Maybe our only real difficulties in growing up together came when I was nearing puberty around thirteen. I'd get the urge to be out by myself in the woods. Maria might be reading. I'd say, "I'm just going out for a short walk". She'd put the book down and straight away appear on the doorstep with me. It wasn't quite like having a pet dog but close.

Either she'd come and I'd sulk. Or I'd tell her I wanted to be by myself and her disappointment would pierce me. Either way the walk was miserable.

Perhaps she sensed I was growing into a world where she wasn't. Causing her all the more to want to tag along with me, reinforcing in me the longing to get out and be alone. It wasn't that I didn't want to be with her. I still loved playing, joking or just going around with her. She'd always know when to be quiet, when to walk along side by side with me crunching twigs and dry leaves while listening to forestry rustles. But now sometimes I just longed to be my myself. To have emotions and thoughts not shared by anyone, to feel myself free and experience the growing strength of my limbs, to be alert and alone in the woods.

Neither of us quite understood what was happening. We both sensed something new reaching into our lives but couldn't find woods for it.

Earlier if there'd been anything the matter with one of us, we'd always gone first to each other. Half a sentence and Maria would somehow get the picture and come out with a cryptic insight to thwack me over the head with, and change the whole perspective. If I were feeling low she'd just come and give me a hug.

And Maria? She was pretty well always okay as long as mother and me were. But if something did happen to hurt her we'd just go out walking or sit together by the fire and elsewhere, and pretty soon everything would be fine again.

Then suddenly lightning ... I wanted to be by myself.

I loved my mother, we both did. She was a good mother who kept us well, kept the home warm and human for us, read us stories around the fire at night ... but there was no doubt, Maria and I went first to each other before anything else in the world.

Martha, my mother, always seemed to carry a hidden sorrow or regret, not on the surface but deeper down. Only now more than thirty years from those times do I begin to perceive that perhaps one of the reasons might have been because she felt she wasn't really needed. That sublime unqualified trust and nearness which children have for their mothers, that brother and sister gave to each other.

There were no other children. Her husband gone. Her wider family nowhere. Our house alone in a clearing in the woods. No lovers took the path to her arms. Few came to visit us.

Had she lived longer, had things gone otherwise, had ... but it is to late. I can only look up to the clouds.

Though there have been moments when alone in a church's silence, pondering if we really do live in a world where saints can intercede for the living and the dead. That I have found myself wondering if I can give her now what was never offered earlier or perhaps she can comfort me today with solace not sought from her before.

Only I don't know how. I don't know how.

11. A Man's Gotta Do ...

In that family crisis arising from my incipient adolescence it was my mother who rescued us. She'd been eyeing us inquisitively for a week or two without saying a word about growing up pains.

One afternoon I'd slunk out of the back door desperate to be alone and just not feeling capable of coping with Maria's expression if I said no to her tagging along with me. For nearly two hours I'd been tramping out in the woods. It was good to feel my arms and legs. I'd climbed trees, run and jumped like an Indian brave, hidden behind tree trunks from imaginary enemies, and cast sticks and stones at pretended wild animals. And now I sensed hunger, honest hunger. The stars were appearing as I pushed open our garden gate. Lights in the kitchen, smoke rising steadily from the chimney.

Even as I closed the gate, I began to realise the effects of my slinking away. Opening the porch door and taking off muddy shoes, I gave a cheery, *Hi, I'm back.*

There was a noise on the stairs. When I came into the kitchen mother was alone.

Hi, where's Maria?

Upstairs.

Everything okay?

She turned from the bubbling food and looked straight at me, *As well as can be expected.*

What's that supposed to mean?

There was a long pause before she answered, *Maybe you'd better go up to her.*

Hmm!

For a minute or two I sat with my chin cupped in my hands, staring at the kitchen table already laid for dinner. Then reluctantly I got up, slammed the kitchen door and trudged upstairs aggrieved that the price tag of Maria's weeping was attached to my private walk in the woods.

I tapped on the door. No answer. Knocked again. A sort of grunt. I opened it. The room was none too light, a star was visible through the window. She was lying face down on the bed. I could already feel resentment evaporating, my lips parting in a smile.

You okay?
No!

I sat down on the bed and gave her sweater a gentle tug.
Let go!
What's the matter?
Headache.
Oh.

I began to tickle her ribs. She flew round thrashing at me wildly with her hands.

Wow! That's some headache.
You snake, sneaking out on me like that!

I tickled her some more. This time she reacted with feet as well as hands. I dashed out of her door shouting, *Mad dog. Help! Mad dog!*

She came flying down the stairs after me and jumped on my back just as I opened the kitchen door. Usually mother either disdainfully ignored our frolics or got angry telling us to remove ourselves. But now she turned from the oven and walked regally toward us.

My dear Lord and Lady!

Maria stopped punching me. We both stared in surprise. Then trying to imitate a cowboy, mother dropped her voice an octave, *When a man's gettin' to be a man, he's gotta have time to be by himself.* And after a short pause added solemnly, *A man's gotta do what a man's gotta do.* Then with a snappy reversal to her usual soprano pitch, *And if you two can't get your hands washed and be sitting smiling at the table in one minute, there'll be no dinner for you at all.*

The whole thing sounded so funny because she couldn't really do a cowboy accent. She'd always kept the melodious Celtic lilt to her voice. Her own mother was born in Ireland. And my mother somehow never managed to speak proper American. They had laughed at Maria and me when we first attended school because of the way we spoke. Though our speech quickly became normalised we still tended to change to our own family dialect at home, adopting many quaint styles and sayings.

12. Braided Memories

Our family bible was the King James Authorised Version, a relic from my maternal grandfather with his Welsh-English Protestant background. His wife, our grandmother, was an Irish Catholic.

There had been problems. They were treated as pariahs from both sides. His Protestant family despised the Catholic faith. My grandmother's family of Irish Catholics distrusted, even hated Protestants especially those with British roots.

Having confessed their love for each other early, they were then forced apart by their families' ire at this prospective match. She rejected a succession of suitors in the hope he would come to her and propose. His procrastinations were tear-laden and anguished, and at times desperate. They endured much silent and lonely heartache over years before that afternoon.

That afternoon when he set off having no preconceived notion of where he was heading and when she, not knowing why, had the sudden urge to ride out.

He called her name as she rode by. And they stood before each other. And once more confessed their love.

And she in her Irish impulsiveness, perhaps being more aware than he of the family noose, said she wished not to end as Ophelia (her favourite aunt had moved in literary circles) and, paraphrasing Denmark's prince, avowed, *Our destinies are not in our families but in ourselves.*

They eloped there and then, both riding on her horse in a direction more or less opposite to where in a few hours the sun would set.

After a few months of marriage, 'to give their families a chance', they returned to visit. She to insults, he to suffer a serious beating.

They moved north, taking what was then a fairly isolated small-holding. Their first child, a boy, died in infancy. Final contact with their families terminated when instead of receiving tearful letters of sympathy, only grim epistles arrived, letters full of the vengeance of the Lord onto the second and third generations for the failure to uphold their respective religions.

An active second child appeared, my mother. The third and fourth children never came because my grandfather was made an invalid through a riding accident. And spent ten years in a wheelchair. Thankfully on this occasion they were spared commiserations from their families.

My grandmother took over the farm as best she could. Though the work was hard and the family impoverished she found the time to read often to her daughter. And also taught her numbers and how to write and read. My mother didn't attend school which partly explains her Irish English in spite of living her whole life in America. At least she didn't go to school until she was placed in an orphanage at thirteen. Grandmother having died with a chest infection, probably pneumonia, about three years after grandfather.

There was an unspoken consensus in the family's religious practices. She took her daughter to the nearby Catholic church. At home they read the King James Bible.

My mother hated her time in the orphanage and never spoke about it. But in spite of its hardships I think their family life was blessed with a certain goodness and contentment. Grandfather's health had been failing over a number of years before he died. It was only with difficulty my mother would speak about him. Though I believe when younger his Welsh tenor was worthy mate for his wife's Irish soprano.

If the mood took her though she could spend half an hour telling us about something done with or for her own mother. Like when they went out and bought a new coat for her twelfth birthday. Or how about a year earlier she knitted in secret a scarf of many colours from left-over wool as a Christmas present for my grandmother. Above all she conjured up for us an impression of that atmosphere around the fire when her mother sang or told stories from the Emerald Isle. Perhaps because she valued this immeasurably, the hearth became the centrepiece of our own home. Where we sat and elsewhered, read or were read to, listened or conversed.

As an adult I remember coming across St. Francis' *Canticle of the Creatures* and reading, "Brother Fire I have always loved you ..." and from somewhere lost within me an essence of those times together around our fireplace welled forth as the opening of a chrysalis.

There were no photographs. My grandfather is for me a vague outline of feeling. A young man grown old who longs to arise and care for his family, a grey grieving in a shrunken form, an impotent anger dwindling into resignation. I see him as he sits in a wheelchair and stares out of the window at his wife and daughter playing together in the open air illuminated by a shaft of sunshine through a cloudy sky.

But through what my mother related, my grandmother has become vividly alive for me. Probably the pictures I have of her bear little resemblance to the way she actually looked. I can see her in my mind around their fire with her young daughter, my mother, on her knees. And when younger I could actually hear her voice inside me as she sang those Irish ballads in my imagination.

The only possessions remaining to my mother when she left the orphanage were the King James Bible, her mother's wedding ring (which had to be sold one Christmas when I was still young) and a braided belt made by my grandmother herself. This belt with its Celtic-like motifs I've held in my hands many times. I imagine my grandmother's nimble fingers plaiting it together while a smile lit her green eyes.

It isn't easy to understand why we didn't hear more about her from my mother's lips. Though today so many years later, I begin to realise that the poignancy, deepening my mother's memories of her own mother, didn't allow her to toss her recollections lightly over the dinner table. A dinner table where me and Maria, so full of ourselves, rarely bothered to ask about her earlier life. Maybe she felt she would keep her reminiscences till we grew up. Or till she held our own children in her arms.

To this day I am unsure if fate's sorest wound to her was her mother dying at thirteen, or … but mulling over these symptoms of her life, the way she must have laid herself down and let go of her spirit at the end becomes more conceivable.

13. Vladimir

My father Vladimir, a young strong Polish-Russian lion, just swept mother off her feet. He built our wooden two-storied house in the woods with his own hands. There had been plans for seven or eight children so neither the girl's room (Maria's) nor the boy's (mine) were small.

What must our little house have been like then – Vladimir all zest and joy in life, Russian folk songs and laughter. My mother's beautiful soprano enchanting her Irish melodies. Little Alexei (me) falling around noisily and Sonia (Maria) asleep in her cot.

I have some remembrances of him: growing to enormous size as he bent over my bed to tickle my nose with his bushy hair; my running along holding on to his hand; him standing me on the table in the garden and counting one, two, three before I leapt trustingly into his outstretched arms.

We had a couple of photographs. The polarity created between these naked, discolouring chemical portraits and my own few vivid glimpses from memory became resolved into living pictures as I listened to occasional stories about him.

These images or imaginings of my father are still inside me somewhere like an underground brook passing timelessly beneath the present – or a fiery ember buried in the burnished lustre of the child within me.

At home when growing up he was rarely mentioned. Again maybe the depth of my mother's feelings mourned him beyond years. And somehow silenced easy talk about those little things that filled the first years of our home with such human warmth. He left too early from my and

Maria's lives. In my mother's heart the linger of grieving for him was veiled by reticence, a reticence which could have been breached. She could have conferred on us stories about her married years, had questions been asked ... but they almost never were.

Vladimir's father was Russian, his first wife Ukrainian. She never made it to America but their child Uri did. His second wife was Polish and Catholic. Here too problems cropped up in their respective Russian Orthodox and Roman Catholic communities. This second wife died while her son Vladimir was still an infant. His father took a third Russian wife. And becoming progressively more orthodox as the years went by set his jaw against his son's betrothal to an Irish orphan.

Vladimir's youthful zeal sounded its own decision. He forsook the birthright of inheritance, the safety net of family connections and swept Martha, my mother and the woman he loved, into his arms and off to the house in the woods he built for her with his own hands; trusting in his own resilience and initiative to solve all problems which might come their way.

He had taken out loans to buy the building materials and the ground, the fairly large garden around our house. And so he needed to earn money. Sometimes he had to work away. He found a temporary job with great pay half a day's drive distant. Only coming home every other weekend. He'd been working there a few weeks when the accident happened. It was over, I believe, in a matter of seconds.

When Vladimir did something he didn't hang back.

After his death there was little coming and going between us and his family. We were left alone. Our

Russian names fell into disuse. And the house of Vladimir and his wife and his children became our home – the garden where me and Maria in the care of his widow, our nanny, played our enchanted play.

14. Uri's Nik

About the only visitor we ever had from the Slavic side of the family was Vladimir's elder half brother Uncle Uri. He was moderately successful in business opening a restaurant called "Uri's". Soon after the first manned space flight he changed the name to "Uri's Nik". But he was careful to keep the Stars and Stripes showing with a portrait of Abe Lincoln and photos of our boys, our astronauts, over the bar. Maybe he could have made piles of dough with a succession of Uri's Niks to rival MacDonalds but he preferred vodka to bank balances. Being more than happy as he was: Uncle Uri the proprietor of Uri's Nik, going around to chat with his customers at their tables.

He lived in the next state. Sent us Christmas and birthday cards and vouchers for presents. But seldom wrote, not because he wasn't too hot on us but because he almost never wrote to anyone. His spirits just wouldn't inscribe in pen and ink. And as our home had no telephone, no electricity, he couldn't ring.

It wasn't often he visited us after his eating place opened. And when he did come to our home it was always unannounced. He hardly ever travelled because holidays, or holy days, were spent celebrating with a glass down at Uri's.

His rotund face always threatened to smile. His clear blue eyes (trusting as a child's, worldly as a Parisian madame's) shielded a humour which loved to make laughter. A laughter which was inclusive in the sense that with him people just laughed together not at somebody else. And if you did happen to be the brunt of one of his jokes, it was like being offered the guest of honour's seat.

People generally felt better after they had laughed a bit with Uncle Uri.

As a kid he'd learnt to play the violin. But as age gave weight to his frame he preferred to dump his gradually waxing preponderance deftly down at the piano. Heavy fingers merging lightly with the keys as Chopin chords melted into the air or as he tinkled popular melodies for the diners at his joint. Occasionally if there were only a few people or if he were alone, he would sit and improvise. His figure bowed over the keyboard swaying gently as to breezes over the steppes, as if an undercurrent rove the never fully resolved dissonances and ever transposing rhythmic themes with the unrest of the continent's longings ... alive even as night reigns above the Russian earth.

At such times you began to realise that though you could hear the irrepressible immediacy in Uncle Uri's voice there was something in him which bore no natural antecedent, an element not encapsulated, a part of him which never really incarnated in America ... where he held court at the Nik: Uri, prince and jester, playing to the guests each of whom was king.

15. Ruskaya

Pricked perhaps by some premonition, my father took out a life insurance a couple of months before the accident. The insurance company, rebelling against the idea of having a young widow and two children round their necks, tried to make out the policy was invalid. Mother was totally distraught and in no position to handle matters. And there was no one to help her.

Not until Uncle Uri appeared and sized up the situation in the time it takes to down a glass. It was only days after the funeral. He had loved my father and felt for us, and knowing he was mother's only hope he took a grip on himself. Putting on an air of carefree joviality he sidled down to the insurance office with a giant bottle of vodka.

With the ruddy open face and heavy accent of a Russian peasant freshly deposited from the steppes, they thought they'd sell him half a dozen dud policies in minutes. Thinking about the lucrative cut he'd get from insuring Uncle Uri's restaurant (though at the time it was only a hamburger stand) against death-watch beetles or oversized hailstones, the manager invited him into the back office for a cosy chat, just the two of them, about the lasting benefits of insurances.

He was prised into taking the first glass by Uncle's flat comment, *Among Russians: no vodka, no deal!*

On finishing their first, Uri gave a chuckle, *The more vodka, the less to hide!*

And so our seller of cast-iron security put his honest-John hand forward and matched Uncle Uri glass for glass.

By the time the bottle was standing three quarters empty on his desk, the manager finally tagged on to just who Uncle Uri was. The immigrant's beaming face and thick accent took extraordinary delight in drawing out the story of the poor widow with two young children and the insurance shark: Pictures, tearful interviews – big news for a local audience. With an air of cherub perched atop of a Baroque fountain, the seller of security stood supporting himself with a hand on his desk while his other held out his glass. Uncle drained the last drops into it. The insurance broker didn't alter his pose, his slightly glazed eyes betrayed the effects of Uri's suggestive conjuring, as he saw himself caught in vindictive profile on the cover of next week's local newspaper, the caption reading: Insurance swindler steals from kids.

As Uncle Uri put the empty bottle down on the desk his confident glow seemed to dissipate. He began wearily to button his overcoat, muttering sadly, *Hopeless! No pity wins.* And he shuffled away, his bowed figure emanating the resignation of a refugee.

Uri's sudden transformation caused the Insurance agent to draw his attention back into the office. Uncle put his hand on the door knob ... maybe the bad dream was about to leave, as it had come, through the door.

No pity wins. The Commerce Man of Venice again, (he'd only ever read Shakespeare in Russian) shaking his head dejectedly Uncle half turned back as he spoke, *No blood in the flesh.*

Profiled to the door's framework Uncle Uri suddenly stiffened and struck out violently to make a graphic display of plunging and twisting; and as he turned the imaginary dagger he hissed in an icy undertone, *Ruskaya!*

The bad dream was creeping back under the bedclothes.

Still framed by the door but now frontal Uncle Uri stood eyes half-closed as if remembering something significant. His words were emphatic, *My grandfather, a tough army surgeon, always said: If a patient's got a fatal illness tell him right out. Uri the Scalpel they called him because he loved doing amputations.*

The refugee, an exile dribbling from the downtrodden and anonymous masses, a candidate for a disappearing Black Maria ... was changing into an interrogator from the Lubijanka. And his stare coming closer loomed over the insurance agent in that claustrophobic vodka-reeking room.

Ruskaya was dragging our broker into an abysmal future.

Two feet away Uri stopped. The shrouded threat abating completely, his gaze becoming filled with profound sadness as he asked, *Do you have a widow?*

The cherub tried to raise his glass to his lips but Uncle dropped a heavy hand on this shoulder, *No insurance against Ruskaya.*

Rus – came the vague response.

Kaya! With 'k' as in cut! Uri drew a muscular forefinger across his victim's Adam's apple. Then curling the same forefinger under the nose of this seller of safety nets for the unfortunate so as to beckon him closer, he bent his own spirit-breathing face to within an inch or two of the other's and whispered, *Ruskaya!* Shooting an ominous glance at the door and making a gesture for them to keep silent, he added in an undertone, *Mafia.* Immediately straightening up, his face bright, his voice booming, *Mafia!* and breaking into a hearty laugh, *Mafia! Russian Mafia!*

He clapped the insurance clerk on the back with such force as to send him sprawling over the desk. The vodka in his glass spilling over a pile of newly signed policies. Dumped on his now disordered work-table, he looked up to see Uncle's broad back and long dark overcoat disappearing through the door.

Some minutes later the secretary's knock brought him out of his stupor, *Excuse me, but there's a man with a camera who says he wants to snap you for the Ruskaya archives; One frontal, one profile ... shall I?*

Uncle Uri had made a detour to the photographer's.

That time, right in the freeze of the Cold War, they'd have believed anything of Russians.

Uri returned the next day with a Russian acquaintance also clad in a dark overcoat, with a Siberian-bear jaw and the squint of someone about to accomplish a KGB contract. He carried a violin case, a heavy one (they'd put a lump of iron in it).

After a sleepless night's trauma the manager was none too perky and whenever the talk dried up Uncle Uri cast a significant glance over to the violin case while his colleague unsmilingly tapped it.

The case of the tapping violin eroded final resistance. And with Uncle hiring a smart lawyer to work out the details, my father's premonition provided for his family.

We received a lump sum big enough to pay off loans for the land and the building materials, so the house and garden were ours. And we were guaranteed a monthly pay cheque. Just enough to keep us given we grew our own vegetables, picked berries, made jam, chopped wood, and were given some help from around the church.

16. Of Song and Story

Our childhood couldn't really have been happier. Though mother might have been better without those grudgingly given insurance cheques, better leaving the house in the woods and marrying again while still young. Who knows, who knows, maybe not, maybe she wasn't so unhappy watching her kids grow and elsewhereing in the evenings over the hearth even if more backwards than forwards. But if she took a break from singing after her mother died, she gave it up for good after losing Vladimir.

She sang in church. But only on very special occasions like around the Christmas tree were we able to cajole her into singing for us. To see a regal sheen on her figure and her countenance as she gave voice to the hallowed depth of a hymn or carol. To sit with my sister on the carpet in front of the log fire looking up at her as she sat in the old armchair, a sparkle leaping from her blue-green eyes as she conjured the blarney or longing from an Irish folk piece, and in the pause at the end of a song a hushed presence echoing in the crackle and warmth of burning wood.

A magician in the art of singing my mother, and knew it, I think, only as Prospero cast away his book – deeper than did ever plummet sound – she buried her song. And maybe if she hadn't her children might never have relinquished faeryland.

A few times after succumbing to our requests to sing for us I heard her later weeping softly but bitterly in her bedroom which adjoined our living room.

If there was a repository of vocal talent in our family only a very meagre portion passed on untransposed to me.

For song, speech, acting – few natural gifts came my way. Maria scooped those birthrights. Not that she sang a lot. Some sense of tact kept her from singing too much at home around mother. But her drama, her storytelling – right from childhood she'd just open her mouth to repeat part of a story, *And he was told to go back deep into the dark forest to find her lost jewel ...* and we'd already be in another world.

It was only years later I became consciously aware that while always retaining her own unique quality, her voice was as protean as her face and her movement – and expressed just as transparently what she felt and who she was.

In earlier years I simply enjoyed talking to her. Or if she told a story, her speech for me would be a stepping stone into the tales. She would often retell stories we'd heard mother read a couple of days earlier. (If I asked her to tell me a story from the day before she'd just say, "It ain't done yet". And I'd tell her to screw the heat up on her story-cooker.) When she retold a tale, I lived in it and didn't take a pace back to observe her way of speaking.

Once though when she was around fifteen I went along with her to baby-sit at the home of the newer neighbours who had also built a house in the woods fairly close to ours, maybe a five minute walk away. They became some of the few real friends my mother ever had. There were three children aged five, seven and eight. Up till then I'd spent very little time with young children and rarely seen my sister around little kids.

Bedtime approached and she of course told them a fairytale. A Russian one I knew well. She sat them cosily around the black iron stove before beginning.

In Russia there are endless, endless forests which make our little woods here seem like a clump of trees. In those forests bears trample, wolves howl, and squirrels hop in the branches.

No different from words anyone else might use. But when she said 'endless' and repeated it, the cosy fireside started stretching away without boundary; the kids huddled together from the loss of their fours walls of comfort.

Then came 'trample' and from her way of saying it you knew it weren't no menacing grizzly but a clumsy honey bear probably wriggling its back-end Pooh-fashion out of a hollow tree. But with 'howl' the wriggle became a shiver. And with 'hop' the squirrel landed nicely with its tail in the usual S-form.

She went on, *Sometimes, if you're lucky, in a clearing among the trees you might find ... well, what might you find?*

The kids, all wide-eyed involvement, blurted out, *A witch.*

A wolf.

A prince.

Ah, maybe. Maybe you might stumble across all of these. But after being lost all day in the forest, cold and hungry, and getting scared as it began to grow dark, you might peep from behind a tree and ... see a woodcutter's dwelling, a little house with a lamp shining in the window and smoke folding and rising from the chimney.

The way she dwelt on, almost tasted the verbs 'peep' and 'see' ... your inner eyes just opened elsewhere. When she said, 'folding and rising', the youngest sort of rolled over forwards.

She continued, *The poor woodcutter had lived there with his wife for years and years but they had never had any children. Then one day ...*

With 'years and years' ordinary sequential time was twisting over, turning round on itself. Her uttering of 'one day' was a kind of magical invocation of a secret, a curtain opening into the chalice of time.

I was split in two, seeing my Maria of fifteen and my little Maria seven or eight years earlier; listening to the story now and remembering how I heard her tell this same fairytale as a child. Part of me was listening to the story and making inner pictures, and another part looking at these little kids in front of me – the very image of how I must have been years before.

They heard the axe chopping the tree and saw the golden circlet sinking into the water; they cried with the little lost princess. How human they were, how human we all were, sitting together by the glow of the stove listening to a fairytale.

Walking back on the narrow path through the wood. Maria in front because she saw better in the dark than me. I was shaking my head, *I'll swear to God, Maria, we ought to have a dozen kids.*

She stopped dead.

But we're brother and sister!

I didn't mean like that. I meant we could open an orphanage or something ... maybe like Holden C. I could catch kids in the rye fields before they hurtle down over a precipice. And bring them back so you can tell them stories.

Mm ... only not twelve, hundreds and hundreds.

I could sense her eyes shimmering in the deep darkness as we pictured our orphanage with its hundreds and hundreds and hundreds of children.

A golden light fell on these couple of years before college. Adolescent crises behind us, adventure everywhere. We still led a kind of double life. At school we were ordinary natural kids – more or less. At home we lived without electricity and thus had no TV, radio, telephone or even electric lights. Maria called the electric lighting in school 'undressing light.' Naked, artificial and not easy to ensoul I suppose she meant. Anyway without the distractions of TV, Hi-Fi, mobiles, game consoles, or computers and with a sort of forest-like quietness around our home we managed to read and to retell for each other many stories, legends, myths from various civilisations. Greek myths, Homer, Virgil, Norse myths, Gilgamesh, Persian and Egyptian legends, stories about the Buddha, Chinese tales, Eskimo and Red Indian lore.

By great fortune we came across the *Ramayana* and the *Mahabarata* and even an abridged version of the stories about Krishna in the *Shrimad Bhagavata*. Around the time we were reading these legends she said something odd.

I was climbing a tree holding on about a person's height above ground and puzzling how to make the next move up. She was leaning against the trunk as she spoke, *There's something of Christ in Krishna, somewhere.*

With the `t' gone missing?

When I made that comment instead of taking it as a joke or a snidy she just grabbed my ankle.

That's it! You've got it! Then she made an upward-downward sweeping movement with her hands bringing them to a stop with her fingers pointing downwards. *Yes Ray! Without a 't' – before he came down!*

When she did this kind of thing I usually changed the subject. (Strangely enough some years later I came across a Central European esotericist who said more or less the same. But that's another story.)

My way of subject changing was to let out a Red Indian whoop and jump down from the tree. I landed badly and had to limp home with her supporting me. Maybe this is why I remember the incident so vividly.

My ankle hurt and I felt her nonsense was to blame so I had another go at her, *What happened to the 'na', the 'n-ah' at the end of the name?*

You're such a weight Ray!

Na – am I? Naaaah! I wasn't going to give in.

She slipped my arm and left me standing with my weight on one foot, pursing her brows as she spoke, *I think it's related to the Amen only it's been turned the other way around. Come down and beginning to rise up again. Krishna's 'na' has gone to on to be the 'Ah-n' of 'Amen.' Something like that maybe.*

If she got one of her insights, opposing arguments weren't so much parried as drafted in to support hers. You'd think you were using a sharp axe to chop down the young sapling of her wayward notion. You'd fell it and cut off its branches. With sweat on your brow you'd gesture to the bare trunk lying on the earth and feeling greatly satisfied with your own philosophical dexterity you'd say, "There!"

She'd nod as if to say 'thank you', and calmly proceed to pick it up and use it to build up the house of her own argument. I daren't even try to imagine how I'd have been thrown about if she'd learnt judo.

It wasn't long after this we got hold of a book with lives of saints. In a footnote to one of the lives we read something like: this life is clearly that of the Buddha under another name. We'd already read legends about Gautama and a selection of Jataka tales. So it was a great and glad surprise to find him in the Calendar. Alas! That same footnote went on to say that he had of course been removed.

Maria was miffed or it might be truer to say pained, real hurt by them getting rid of Buddha. She went about with a cross face for a couple of days after this, not her usual thing at all. When I asked what the matter was, she said she'd been thinking about Gautama and that maybe the writers of the 'life' had known more than the 'correctors.'

Good job we weren't living in the Middle Ages or they'd have burnt her for sure.

That was one of Maria's problems, well perhaps not a problem, a trait. She couldn't compartmentalise. Well, maybe she could but she wouldn't rest content with it. Buddha and Christianity, you'd think they were separate realms. But not for her.

I was a natural-born compartmentaliser. I could do physics for instance, think in terms of atoms and electrons, and never wonder what that had to do with leaves opening in Springtime or Sunday service. Whereas she would probably want to know what nuclear chain reactions had to do with angels.

She didn't go round asking that kind of thing in school. Ours was a Catholic school but it wasn't that Catholic.

Even though she wouldn't ask teachers she'd ask me. And we'd stroll around Aquinas' conundrum about how many angels can dance on a pinhead in a more contemporary setting: How many angels can pop through a proton.

Maria once said she didn't believe in protons. She said all that breaking down into electrons, neutrons, particles and so on, only had to do with nature breaking up. That it wasn't nature as she was out there in the woods but only nature when you put high-voltage charges to her, twisted her, tortured her, split her up or went nature-smashing by using a cyclotron's enormity against her. And that those atomations and electronicity were only to do with nature having the cramps.

I thought that was great. The ideal opener for the next physics lesson. So as soon as it was about to begin I put my hand up from the back bench in the lab and said, or at least I intended to say, "My sister says all this atoms, electrons and radiation stuff is just nature having the cramps."

Only somehow it didn't come out like that. I'll swear I never intended it but the last two words got changed to, 'a crap.' Needless to say the class laughed. Miss Smythe-Blethem, the physics teacher, was not amused. I mean she could have made a joke of it. She could have said something like, "Cut the constipations" or something. But she just stared.

All I got for trying to brighten up the start of a lesson was the even-numbered exercises on page such and such for extras. She also sent me down to see Morris in Room 17. He gave me the odd-numbered exercises on the same page to go with them. Visits to Room 17 were usually worse so I can't complain.

Miss Smythe-Blethem? Well, I don't know if she was young or old. But she was, as the English say, about the most po-faced person imaginable and she wore oversized fashion glasses.

A couple of months after this, the funniest thing happened. Jolly found a vibrator in the physics storage room. He asked Miss Smythe-Blethem what this equipment got put into. And before she could give him an answer he proceeded to do a pretty good impersonation of somebody being given an electric shock.

And he wasn't even sent to dance with old Morris in Room 17.

Where did I come from? Oh yeah, clerical correctness, out with the Buddha. Funny maybe I've sort of unconsciously taken a lesson from the cardinals; you start with bishoprical political correctness, make your exclusions ... yet somehow in the end it always comes round to deviations in the bedroom.

I wonder if Miss Smythe-Blethem would need to go to confession if she put a rubber on her vibrator?

When I was away at college Maria wrote me a letter which said something like: "Maybe it's okay they shoved the Buddha out of the Roman Calendar because maybe his help is needed more by Fundamentalists and other Christian Get-Outers. Those who don't say they want out from wheels of birth and death but say they 'want up', to get up there to the good life with their friends and relatives. Those who think they can get up there by saying 'Lord, Lord' without taking a path of renunciation and spiritual striving as do faithful Buddhists. Maybe Gautama can teach the Fundamentalists there's more to it than ranting, 'Lord, Lord!' from their pulpits. Anyway when

Gautama was here, wanting out would be the same as wanting to get back to Him as it was before He came down. But after His sorrowful way, He's with us here. So why do those Fundamentalists want out? Why don't they want to work with Him, work here with Him for all that is good and human. Why do they just want out?"

Cryptic? Maybe, but if she were being philosophical most of what my sister said or wrote was tough to put into boxes. She was Roman Catholic but she loved the Buddha and Krishna.

Funny how if you look at the so-called Christian Right and to those who talk a lot about going 'up there' and who speak of down here as a bit of tribulation to be got through before going up, you see how most of them don't seem to be short of a dime or two. I mean if down here isn't such a big deal, how come most of them seem to have access to big bucks?

Anyway where did I come from? Oh yeah, books, legends, literature. We didn't miss out on our Christian European roots: the Desert Fathers, Celtic saints, *The Way of a Pilgrim,* (somehow we always kept up our lives of the saints) then there were the Arthurian legends, Tristan, Wolfram's (and Chrétien's) Percival stories, Grail legends, *Don Quixote* – which was fun to set beside Mallory.

Once we were in the garden digging up some potatoes when an Air Force jet flew fairly low over us. I asked Maria if it wouldn't have been a help to have had one of those to reconnoitre the Castle of the Grail.

She answered tersely, *Gardening is closer to the Grail than air raids and cyclotrons.*

She wasn't too hot on cyclotrons, my sister.

Maybe this was only a youthful flight of fancy but as we were nearing the end of *Le Morte D'Arthur* we made a promise to each other to seek the Grail together. Maria said even if we got separated, as always seems to happen to those seekers, we should still seek for the Grail together in our separation.

I have always remembered that promise. Even now rarely a week goes by without my wondering in earnest what the quest for the Sangreal may signify in our time. At the very least this has led me to question my compartmentalisations.

Looking back it seems to me my sister always tried to overcome whatever compartmentalisations she encountered. She strove to comprehend history and life around us in relation to Christianity, that deeper river of Christianity which poetically we might call the Quest for the Sangreal.

And I wonder sometimes if this is not the middle way to be found between the undiluted spirit of the Desert Fathers who lived with heaven by heaven for heaven and who truly gave little thought to down here; and that of the bishops who think Christianity is a matter of behaviour, of getting people socially adjusted enough to follow religious rules.

In setting out this polarity with holiness on one side and social Christianity on the other then maybe the solution, the higher synthesis, is implicit. Not the lukewarm spectre where the pole of fire is mixed with that of water, not compromise where the flame of the sacred is diluted down to become religiously acceptable behaviour. But where holiness is to be found not only in seclusion or in the sacred Mass , it is also present in active life.

This is Sacramentalism.

That which is done here is raised up there. That which is intended there is realised here.

But we need the key to unite heaven and earth ... the Chalice ... to be found not only within ecclesiastical sanctuaries.

There were twelve around Him yet the Church was founded only upon one. Or as my sister once said, *Religion is only one twelfth of Christianity.*

But I'm digressing too far. Let me come back to our teenage reading. We managed some novels *Bleak House, Catcher in the Rye,* (titles Maria liked) but our favourite was unquestionably *Lord of the Rings.*

This story set in the Middle Earth which though of the author's making didn't feel made up. You know how sometimes you meet someone for the first time, only you're sure you've met or known them before. They're familiar, they couldn't be anyone else. Or maybe if you're listening to say one of Mozart's late piano concertos for the first time you can't guess the next theme but when it comes you realise it had to be like that, it had to be those notes and not any others.

Even if not raised to full consciousness the same intimations came to me when we read this adventure. I seemed to know the story already yet for me it was new. As we read I had no notion what would happen next yet when the events came about, I felt that what took place had to be.

Even if fiction, *Lord of the Rings* bore the hallmark of fairytale: that quality of not being man-made (or, as Tolkien might have said, the quality of being sub-created).

Years of experience have shown me people find this book when they stand most in need of it. With some in adolescent crises, with others as the meaning in their lives is drying up, some in the aftermath of a break-up or a loss. Others read the book early in life but only at a second reading perhaps many years later does a secret gate stand ajar in their consciousness which allows them to unite with the adventure.

On a certain level Tolkien's novel knocked me out of my senses or perhaps I should say knocked me back into my senses, or maybe better put: bore me through my senses. I was shaken and began to see nature anew.

I'd grown up with the woods about me, delighted in their scents and presence and in crunching frozen leaves on frosty mornings. I'd lived within the seasons as they changed. Nature had always been natural to me and I'd loved her. But through this book, as if smitten by Galadriel's glance, nature became supernatural. She regained the quality of being enlivened. I looked anew at twilight through the trees, seeing the sky's pale illumination and wanted to hold on to it, breathe and be alive in it. Through descriptions of elven light in Tolkien's Middle Earth I learnt again Nature's magical transparency.

Under twilit or starlit boughs I knew how to rekindle my sight outside myself and experience nature as imbued with elven or ethical ether.

Maybe reading this with Maria allowed these qualities to come alive for me. I would read it aloud. But before this she would retell the narrative of two day's earlier then we would talk about what had happened in the reading of the day before. Only then would I read the new part aloud.

Doubtless my sister didn't need reminding of an elven sight (of that quality of empathy in Tolkien's beings who are 'far more natural than men') for her to be able to live in nature's blossoming and withering. After all a little kid who saw butterflies swimming in light, probably even in her teens still swayed with the engendering dances of Natura Naturans. (Nature in her creating, in her invisible weaving of life, in the activity of her unseen forces which bring the potential into the actual.)

But me coming eighteen, playing football, handling a baseball bat ... I was already clumsily cracking beneath my feet the dry branches of Natura Naturata. (Nature as created, surface nature, materialised nature.)

Through this book I found nature again. The nature about me I was losing without realising it.

Sort of like being married to a woman for ten years and taking her totally for granted. Then some guy comes up, grabs you by the shoulder and says, "Hey man, you've got a smasher of a woman!"

"Me? Really, you think so?"

And you take a fresh look.

No longer afraid of night in the woods, at least not when we two were together, we walked out under the stars: composing tunes and singing lays of the Middle Earth. We peered through branches at the twinkling heavens and stood upon the scented earth. We looked upon our lake and called it 'Mirromere' and saw the loveliness of starry night reflected in its water.

Story was new, and newness now.

17. Of Endings and Beginnings

Some years ago (how many – well roughly the time it takes a babe to grow to procreative age) I started to write about life with my sister with the intention of taking my biography up to the present. That present is now thirteen years gone. And we've all entered a new millennium.

Most of my adult life I've written articles for newspapers and magazines but have never come to grips with writing a real book. In my naivety I thought my vague notion of contents would go to make an average-sized book. I now realise this was an underestimate. If everything had gone in, the finished product would have made *War and Peace* look like a short story.

Thus I have had to break it up. But linear time (or narrative) is hard to keep hold of when you're alive. Some things which happened way back seem to have kinship with what is near. If I'd been dead it would have been a lot easier to have done straight narrative year by year. Then again if I were dead the book would probably never get written.

Maybe in the final analysis linear or narrative time is more appropriate for biography than autobiography. And anyway, even if I managed to keep myself in line, how could I do that with Maria – if anybody is alive she is.

There you see, I should by all conventions be employing the past tense but it comes out in the present!

What was I trying to say, ah yes, endings. I've written something and it's got to come to a halt or at least a pause. Only everything is up in the air! Have I reached my late teens or am I still in earlier childhood?

There's Jolly, there's old Morris in Room 17, Uncle Uri, M66, Sister Anna's stories, Father Jerome, Father Rufus, Gina and Enrico. Gina and Enrico, shucks! I haven't got that far yet or perhaps you could say I've already passed them by since we met them early in our lives.

Somewhere or other you've got to call it a day and maybe this is as good a place as any. In the next part I promise to follow a more stringent narrative approach. Well, since I can't turn one white hair black nor one black hair white, not promise; let's just say, I shall have the intention to make do with sequential time ... and if at the end of the second part I find myself in the same position of having to apologise for jumping about ... all I can say in my defence is that it's hard to put what's alive into boxes of time.

There you see again. I use the present when it should have been the past or was it the future tense?

Why does our present get so mixed up with our past?

Didn't a wise man say – oh sorry, it was my sister in one of her crypticisms. I was moaning about something I can't remember what, when she exclaimed, *Ray! Don't you know that if the past doesn't get involved with your present you'll never make it to your future.*

> ... to be continued ...

Interlude Between Part I and II

(The reader is free to spring over these philosophical musings and get right on with the narrative in Part II.)

Now as I look back to my childhood home, it seems to me that the companion of our evening time together, the living log fire, has an exact counterpart for families in the late Twentieth Century household.

We sat and watched the fire's ever-changing flames and were together within its atmospheric warmth. We saw living pictures in our imaginations of what we daydreamed, read or heard. We spoke and listened. And, though in our home this only happened occasionally, we sang.

In the latter part of the twentieth century the log or coal fire was replaced by the multimedia machine: TV, computer, Hi-Fi, game console in the corner of the lounge. That familiar atmosphere around the flames has became the shimmer and flicker of the screen which each of us has our attention drawn toward. The pictures in our imaginations have been replaced by outer images on the screen, the songs we sang have become sounds from loudspeakers.

The same functions are performed. Yet when I think of these things I cannot help conjuring in my mind a balcony where a man stands above a busy marketplace, his voice calls down to the people, "New lamps for old! New lamps for old!"

His sales ploy's catchy, his voice eager yet soothing. His lamps are shiny, fashionable, it's just so easy to exchange the old battered lamp, I've always had, for a new one. But his lamps are all outer glitz. Just as the screen is all surface.

Of course there's something behind the surface of a screen, a huge sophistication of electrical engineering, software and broadcasting. But the process is the same whether you're seeing a jingle to advertise cat food, computer-generated images of a toy's story, a nature program or pictures of maimed children from a war zone. The process behind it and the screen pictures are totally disconnected.

The image on the screen being but coloured dots updated 60 times a second.

The old lamp is magical. There is something inside which can be released.

Why is it that I can look at a real landscape and be deeply moved yet on another occasion I see the same landscape in similar conditions and am untouched by it?

The usual explanation is that it's subjective: Beauty is in the eye of the beholder. What I feel is not due to what is out there but what's in me, where 'in' is in some vague sense supposed to mean inside my skin or brain.

Is this an explanation or a cop out, an explaining away instead of an explanation?

Examine yourself next time you look at a landscape and are unmoved by it and see if it isn't so that in this instance the feeling really is: the landscape is out there, I am here separate from what's outside me.

But do the counter exercise as well. Next time you experience your heart moved by nature, by a sunset or a tree – isn't it so that you are out there within what you see and breathe?

Not convinced? Well, don't you realise that physicists and neurologists have 'proved' you can't hit a baseball! And by analogy you can't return a serve.

You think Agassi could return a Sampras serve? No way! It aced him every time. Pete didn't need to move in because even a second serve whizzed past Andre, every single time. Didn't quite happen like that you say? Don't you realise Agassi is demolishing the Kantian world conception each time he returns a serve! This is a very serious business, Agassi acting as agent provocateur against the Kantian universe.

And what's that about Mr. Strawberry ... blowing raspberries at the Kantian status quo.

The Kantian universe? In normal scientific mode it could be described thus: Out there is something; light reflected from this something goes into my retina; this causes a chemical reaction which creates nerve impulses which go through my nervous system to the brain where these impulses are then 'processed' (my 'I' is thought of as being somehow in this processing, this conjuring up of pictures corresponding to the outer world) then other nerve impulses are sent to arms and legs and eyes in order to get them to move.

The server hits the ball. But time passes with all that retina, nerve and brain business so when 'I' see him hit it, the ball is already flying half way across the court. When 'I' see the ball half way down the court, time has already elapsed and the ball is about to bounce. 'I' send nerve messages to my arms and legs telling them to move right. But by the time these nerve messages are translated into the chemical processes that move the muscles the ball has already gone past me.

So you see, 'I' just can't return a tennis ball, it's impossible! Ergo when Andre returned a Pistol Pete second serve (not to mention a first serve) the Kantian universe was blown away.

What does this mean? Firstly, it means that 'I' am not only in my brain and nervous system. There is just not enough time to turn nerve impulses into bodily movements. I am in my muscles, my blood, my whole body. (And isn't it so that nerve impulses allow me to sense muscular activity rather than bring my muscles into movement?)

Secondly, it means when I see something, this seeing is not an arcane process sitting on top of electro-chemical reactions somewhere between nerve messages from the retina and the neural networks of the cortex; it means that when I see something, I am really out there in what I see – I am in my sight, in my very seeing of the physical world. The Greeks knew this two and a half millennia ago and called it the 'tactile arm' from the eye.

It's just that last century's old man's modernist science (with the emphasis on old and man – what's that? – no, I did not put the adjective dirty in front!) and today's old man's technology have forgotten it.

Kant is from the Eighteenth Century.

The philosophical underpinnings of so-called modern science are blown away, like a stack of cards hit by a Federer smash, whenever Djokovic returns a serve.

The Kantian philosophical underpinnings of modern science are only a candle in a gale. (But don't go telling our normal scientists or they might get abnormal seizures.)

Thirdly, it means when we create an imaginative picture we are not in the physical but in the imaginative world. Or as Maria might have said, "We are elsewhere".

So now you know what the 'new lamps for old' slogan really implies, it intends to chain you to the sense-perceptible world, nay more, to bind you to the 'surfaces' of a man-built multimedia existence.

Butterflies Swim in Light

Part II

1. Making Faces

I'm now in my forties and yet in all the multitudes of diverse human beings, I've come across on my travels, I have never encountered another like Maria whose face was her feelings.

Usually peoples eyes brighten or cloud as they react simultaneously with their transient whims and perceptions. Features are more fixed. As age moulds tissue into matter we go around set in our own soberly recognisable looks.

The mature face is a portrait printed in flesh.

Maybe it's because in growing older we forget the need to forget. Well-primed reflexes in familiar situations substitute for wonder's shy awakening. Wonder stirs in that very moment when the ordinary is sent to sleep.

An adult's ingrown attitude is too cushy to uproot, a daytime me too pervasive to retreat from.

In childhood the night's duration leaves yesterday a season away, makes morning into Springtime. (Once it was as tough to come up with the day before, as today to recall what befell us last Fall.)

Or perhaps, as years pile up, the imaginative middle-ground between awareness and wanting erodes. Wishes dissociate from what we do. Fantasy isn't followed into dream. Musing dwindles into dress rehearsals for a humdrum day.

That pinnacle where the princess waits becomes just one more tower block on a post-mod sky-rise.

Inner responses still lighten or dim irises but smiles tend to turn up from habit and tears only come in emergencies.

When young our teddy bear sits down to fresh air tea and paper buns. And the conversation's anything we want to chat about. Our wooden puppet's playtime is unpredictable.

In middle-age a person's pruned back to the role.

An executive doing business by timetable: Meetings, phone calls, emails – all tightly scheduled. Sales psychology (and promotion prospects) prowling around polite and practised exchanges.

An adult's adolescent angst jammed between the alarm clock and the headache pill.

Childlike immediacy a castaway on sleep's silent surge.

But for what we get up to by daytime, the accustomed face is on.

Children can turn what's being experienced into an effervescence of expression. When a smile comes over them everything's sunny and when they cry there's no holding back.

But youthful lips and cheeks as babies' hands are chubby, not fully shaped, not quite stuffed out with self. (When seeing a toddler curling up toes, clenching and unclenching tiny fists, I'm often reminded of a hand being stretched in a small-fitting rubber glove.)

Maybe an adult profile is pressed out personality but well, just trying doing what I've done many times. Try to perceive faces without eyes. Look at somebody in a shop or café and imagine away their eyes, imagine their eyes blank like a statue from ancient Greece – and then see if what's moving them inside is still visible.

As a teenager Maria's face wasn't unformed like a child's, nor formed and finished like an adult's but alive for her immediate experiences. Even when absorbed in something her expression might be still but never static.

And her whole figure flowed in consonance with her facial glows and resolves as the silken contours of a Grecian dancer's dress.

When sad she would sink a little from everywhere. When excited her four limbs (or five if you counted the arching glide of her neck) would splay slightly in all directions as if resonating with an inner musical fervour.

This tendency only subdued as she grew older. It never really left her. Well into her teens when seeing some old Laurel and Hardy comedy in the movies' dark burring, I'd have to put my hand on her shoulder to keep her seated.

Or at about the same age if we stopped by at church – me sitting near the back to take in its silence, she kneeling before the altar or the Lady Statue whispering a devotion and then remaining motionless, so still and upward seeking she almost seemed to be floating. At times I'd find myself staring just to be sure she wasn't hovering above ground like some Medieval saint. I could have stayed beholding her for hours, though probably we were never in more than a few minutes. And I guess most of my time was spent watching her instead of doing my own prayers. When leaving, my conscience would nudge me and I'd glance a little shamefacedly across at the Lady Statue as if to say: my offerings are with my sister's.

As to why Maria's heart shone through her face and figure, the only answer I've ever been able to come up with is that when she experienced something, all of her felt it. What caught her attention occupied her completely.

Bending over a forest flower her faintly open mouth was almost an image of a bud awakening to blossom.

Empathy kindled by a sense of wonder.

Once she got me to play snowflakes ...

2. Flaking Out

She'd have been about four. Outside our home in the woods, afternoon light starting to fade, snow gently falling. I'd gone in for something but she'd stayed out to be with the snow.

Look at her!

Mother's shout brought me scurrying into the kitchen. I grabbed a stool and clambered up to get a peep at my sister through the window; her clothes were all covered in white at the front.

She seemed to be dancing then she ran and leapt forward, opening arms and legs, her body nearly horizontal. Snow puffed up at her landing.

That's twice! What on earth's got into her? With a disbelieving frown mother turned to me, *For goodness go and get her in before she breaks something.*

She was vainly knocking the window at my sister as I pulled on my boots. Shutting the door behind me I skipped the couple of wooden steps leading down to the garden and stopped.

Woodland noises were muffled as the quietness of evening settled with the falling snow. It was almost like being in a snowfall for the very first time. Maria was some yards away with her back to me, rolling and tilting her head like a flake on the tumble. My feet crunched through deeper layers of snow, *Pretending to be Bambi on ice?*

She spun round as though unaware of my approach and seemed for a moment to be taking in what I'd said. Then her lips pursed decidedly, *I was being a snowflake!* She pointed upwards, *See how they stick out arms and legs as they float down.*

I glanced up. A big flake plopped on the tip of my nose. Maria burst into belly laughter and collapsed. It was easy to join in when she laughed. I sank down near her.

The snowflake put her arms round you.

My nose got a cold cuddle.

Ray, lie down and let me roll you into a snowman.

I ploshed a handful of fresh snow on wavy hair popping out from under her woolly hat. She shook her head and blew so that snow sprayed into my face. When I got to my feet she was a few paces away beckoning to me.

Together we watched gently falling snow. It really did seem to glide on downy feelers. I took off my glove and held my hand out to touch its purity. And whispered, *Little snow-feathers*.

Maria responded by tipping her head back as if half expecting to glimpse a giant snow-bird up there moulting.

Her look of surprise gave way to a twinkling expression. With a little tap on my chest she excitedly exclaimed, *Let's play snow-feathers*.

Then she ran, jumped and splayed out just as before, even spiralling around in mid-air so as to bring me into view. I could have sworn she came down slowly, almost as if the snow-filled air magically offered her support.

Something urged me to go and do the same. I charged down a slight incline and flung myself into a free-fall, a couple of feet above ground I shouted and it really felt, *Grea-t!*

The final plosive coincided with the slam, the fluffy top layer thin, the snow below crisp and compact.

How did the landing feel – well, imagine a cross between belly flopping from a springboard and a soccer ball kicked into the crotch.

With the wind knocked out of me no breath came even to cry out. In such moments you forget you're a child.

Maria called my name and cast herself down beside me. No part of my body would move, my eyes were closed. She shook my jacket. A sharp gasp from my lips and somehow I was able to draw breath again. Painfully focusing, her brown eyes next to mine, her cheek resting on the snow. My limbs becoming free to move began to tingle and ache. Tears welled up in me. She threw off her mitts and clasped my hand. I wanted to tell her something I couldn't quite bring to mind but only sobbing came. The pain grew worse.

Then after a few moments started to ease. Maybe only intensified seconds had elapsed since my fall. I was crying. And carried on even after the worst hurt let up. Somehow it felt okay to cry. And to be me again, a little kid with my sister.

Mother rushed out of the house with her old moccasins on, one stuck fast in the snow causing her to tumble headlong before reaching us.

Later sitting around the warmth of the hearth we realised each of us had fresh grazes on our faces.

3. Picture Bibles

From before I was born Father Jerome had been the priest at our church. He was pleasant enough in his own way, I suppose, but well sort of distant and old; he took no part in our childhood except when we attended Mass. He was just a formal part of the church service we simply took for granted.

Right after the business with M66 he got sick or something and was sent away. Local priests helped out with daily Mass and the Bishop even turned up two Sundays running. Father Rufus came as Summer leaves were yellowing.

Looking back our new priest would probably have been in his mid or late thirties: Medium height, short dark hair already showing strands of grey.

If you chanced to see him by himself, you couldn't help sensing a quality of mourning in him as though inside he harboured a hurt or sunder.

But if you spoke to him that grey dwindling sadness in his eyes disappeared into a blue light. He became attentive and alive with a most ungrown-up unpredictability. He could change subjects or moods as effortlessly as an excited adolescent but always there was a part of him that was grown up. Well not grown up, mm, I'd almost say aged or better ageless, ageless yet hidden somewhere near. Maybe it would be true to say he bore a wisdom. But to meet a human being wise in even one field of life is a rare event.

At any rate we liked him, more than liked him. And he seemed to mean a lot to mother too for she was always baking for him. We'd never had so many cookies around the kitchen. He came to our home and ate with us a couple of times soon after moving here. Then he stopped visiting us. It didn't matter much though because mother was always trudging off to the church with something for him or just to help out and clean.

And church services changed. The part where the priest stood up over the Bible and began the sermonising was no longer accompanied by a sense of sinking while a voice detached from personality droned on and while the clock's minute finger pretended to be the hour hand and we'd be wishing to be elsewhere, somewhere, anywhere away from grown-up time.

For one thing Father Rufus spoke less – or maybe moments just moved in a different tempo. And you listened perhaps because you could see what he was talking about.

Perhaps a few weeks after Father Rufus' arrival we were outside one morning, an Autumn wetness over the woods. I'd broken off a leafless branch and was wondering whether it mightn't make a better wizard's staff than a sword. Maria making marks in the mud with her foot, a musing note in her voice as she spoke, *Do you, d' y' think Father Rufus has lost something?*

I immediately pictured him with that pained expression. *Well, he sure seems struck by missing-something misery sometimes.*

We walked around trying to figure out what he might have lost. At first we thought about things, objects. Had he mislaid a prayer book or a crucifix, his Bible maybe?

I threw a twig as I spoke, *It can't really be a Bible, why should he worry about a Bible, all Bibles are the same.*

Maria gaped, then came on at me as if I'd stamped on her figures. *They're not!* Her face screwed up as though she might either punch me or run away in tears behind the bushes. *They aren't the same! Father Jerome's Bible's just got words in but Father Rufus has pictures in his.*

As she spoke I couldn't help thinking of Father Jerome bald and bulky in the pulpit. When he read up or preached words moaned over our heads and time was torture. When Father Rufus told us stories from the Bible we saw them. Samson clothed in skins holding the white jaw-bone of an ox, we saw him as in flesh and blood. Or Jacob lying with a stone for a pillow under a starry night sky.

With Father Jerome preaching, we sat fidgeting in the pews. When Father Rufus spoke about the Sower, you'd see grains of corn scatter on the ground, a greedy yellow-beaked blackbird pecking up some of them, and you'd picture the first tiny see-through green leaves growing forth from the good soil.

When Father Rufus told Bible stories they were as gripping as fairytales – can you imagine that, a story from the Bible as exciting as a fairytale!

Maybe my sister was right, maybe they did have different Bibles. Anyway I wasn't going to make her more upset. *Okay, okay Maria, next time we're in church we'll take a peep.*

Next day mother took us with her to give Father Rufus freshly baked bread. We managed to slip away and sneak into the church through the main doors. It wasn't a big church as churches go, I guess. But we always felt small when we entered, very small and shy in its stillness.

To the left of the altar was the Lady Statue in unpainted wood. Without a whisper we walked slowly up to the pulpit on the right. The huge Bible was open. I could just see its printed sentences, and carefully turned over page after page. Maria on tiptoes holding on to me at first then climbing up me.

No pictures only words and words and words.

Sitting around the table after our evening meal, we asked mother if some Bibles had pictures in. Her whole expression brightened.

I'd have been about your age Ray, maybe a bit older. My mother took me to an exhibition of illustrated Bibles, manuscripts with Biblical events painted by hand.

Even though we seldom asked, we did love to hear about the grandmother we'd never met. We hadn't even a photo of her but when mother spoke about her, I couldn't help seeing her. And I always saw her the same way.

Mother was telling us about herself at that exhibition. A little girl rushing from exhibit to exhibit peering through glass cases holding priceless manuscripts. And asking if they had just the one picture or were full of them.

I was entranced by those brightly coloured paintings, hundreds and hundreds of years old, and there were maybe illustrations on every other page. And those Bibles were so thick with so many paintings. I stood thinking about all those monks writing out page after page by hand, year after year, and drawing and colouring far, far better than I ever could.

I think my mother saw so vividly in her mind the memories she was speaking about that we couldn't help seeing the scenes before us too. A master storyteller was my mother.

We'd been sent to clean upstairs. I was in the doorway of my sister's room. She was sweeping, the handle of the brush a foot above her head.

Do you really think Father Rufus lost an old picture Bible?

She bowed her head and shook it sadly.

What did he lose then? It didn't feel like a game any more, my voice was in earnest. I dearly wanted to know.

Maria looked straight up at me, *His brother?*

What she'd said seemed to shock her. The broom fell from her hand. She ran over and buried her face in my chest. As I mumbled, *Or his sister?*

We hugged each other tightly, unable to bear the unbearable thought of someone losing their only sister or only brother.

The same evening mother told us a fairytale about a prince whose princess was stolen from him. He was given a ball of magic wool which rolled along by itself. His task was to follow the thread though thick and thin until he found his lost princess.

Tears trickled down my sister's face when she listened to the part where the princess was forcibly taken away. It was as always so easy for her to get right inside a fairytale. All at once she did something she hardly ever did when hearing to a story. She turned to me, tears still in her eyes, but I could see she wanted to say something. Her face and figure were trembling slightly.

After the story mother went out into the kitchen to make us a warm goodnight drink. Maria half-sitting, half-lying in the armchair and gazing into the fire. I took hold of her forearm with both hands and whispered, *What was it? Why did you look at me during the story?*

I saw, well not saw, I just knew, I knew it.
Knew what?
I knew what Father Rufus had lost.
What?
His princess.

We didn't get more time to talk just then because mother came in with a night-cap.

Soon afterwards we two went upstairs to bed, me holding a candle. Maria's door came first. I pushed it open. The flame nearly died then grew, burning brightly to lighten the dark. Her bed neatly made, a lived-in feeling nestling in the candlelight; you knew she slept and dreamed here.

After having used my candle to get the one on her bedtable to light, I kissed the top of her head and went a bit reluctantly toward my own room a little further down the hallway.

Our house was made mostly of wood, a real homely home but it creaked, especially at night.

I opened my door. The room was full of shadow. It was larger than my sister's and lacking that welcome always present in hers. Timidly I trod inside trying to look at the flame and not to think of the shapes moving on the walls. After I placed the candlestick on my bedtable the shadows steadied.

My sister was right behind me. I hadn't heard her following. She crept up on the bed and pulled a blanket around her. I was always glad to have her come in to me especially when it was cold and dark.

I sat down on the bed beside her and spoke softly so mother wouldn't be able to hear us, *Maria?*
What?

I don't think a priest can have a princess.

She gave me a queenly look, *Father Rufus did.*

We tried hard but couldn't think of any priest with a princess. We'd never heard of celibacy and even if we had, we wouldn't have known what it meant.

We decided we needed to ask.

After next day's evening meal, sitting around the hearth, wood had been piled on high, mother sitting on my right prodded the fire with a poker. A flame shot up, suddenly died, smoke rose in thick velvety curls. Then the fire crackled and darting flames appeared.

Maria her back to me standing on my left, with her arms and her whole body she tried alternately to imitate flames and then the rolling rising smoke.

Me crouched in the middle, mother gazing into the glowing centre of the fire, the poker resting in her hand. Most of the time she looked like mother but the firelight this evening caught her with teenage wistfulness.

My sister glanced back over her shoulder and gave me a now-it's-time look.

Er, do er priests have, em-

Mother turned absent-mindedly toward me.

Princesses, my sister finishing the question for me, the pitch of her voice at least an octave over mine.

I asked again shyly, *Can a priest have a princess?*

Mother's jaw dropped, she was reddening or maybe it was just colour from the flames. The poker slipped from her hand. She stood up sort of flustered trying to press creases out of her apron, *No, er no, of course not.* Her voice taking on more than usual Irish lilt, *How on earth could you imagine such a thing?*

We were sent up to tidy our rooms.

That Father Rufus would never be able to find a princess made us both down. Maria especially went about moping most of the next day. Walking back from school she pushed up against me and without looking up muttered, *Where do you suppose his princess is?*

Shaking my head, *Dunno.*

We shuffled along the dirt path, twigs brushing against us. The weather overcast, sounds of water dripping, damp dank scents of Autumn, dark blotches on yellow leaves, Summer warmth distilled into the soil. The Fall, Mother Nature in mourning. The loss or sadness of a priest harboured in two children.

I walked by myself and with my sister, we did not speak.

We were maybe half-way home, our moods and the clouds beginning to lighten, when my sister stopped suddenly, put a hand to her mouth, bounded or danced a few paces forward and jumped up spinning round in mid-air to land facing me, her eyes shining, *Maybe, maybe she's in heaven.*

I tried unsuccessfully to snap my fingers. *Yeah, perhaps that's why he became a priest.*

This brought us a real sense of relief.

Which lasted until the next time we chanced to see Father Rufus. Standing midway between the church and the presbytery, head lowered and motionless, an air of unending sadness over him.

4. Giggle and Guffaw

In town shortly after this we bumped into Mrs Lucellini, Enrico the Heretic's wife. Sporting a navy blue costume over her Neapolitan middle-aged spread, she'd just come out of the hairdressers, slouching and puffing over heavy shopping bags.

We two were playing tag outside the adjoining hardware store. Looking back over my shoulder as I was being chased by my sister, I hadn't noticed Mrs Lucellini and ran straight into, well, between her curves.

Raymondino! She let go of her bags and gave me a big hug. I was out of breath from the game and a bit dazed from the bump. The curves came close to suffocating me.

Mother appeared from the hardware store. Mrs Lucellini purred into greetings. Her Italian-American accent chiming one word rapidly into the next.

Light-headed and staggering away from the clinch I caught sight of my sister, her hand lifted and limply motioning toward the women. I turned around but the sun was shining brightly behind them, so I had to put up my hand and duck down slightly to see properly. There was something different about Mrs Lucellini. The hair! Her usual floppy Italian-momma look was gone. Instead her hair was combed backwards finishing high up behind the back of her head and lacquered to stay in place, the ends highlighted with blonde streaks.

A bit like as if someone had struck off the butt of a strutting mini ostrich and stuck it on her for a wig.

Maria was doing her best not to burst out laughing but on the point of losing out. My belly sympathetically contorting with the sniggers, in a last attempt to put off the inevitable I rammed my forearm into my mouth. The tensions in my gut making me splutter and snort.

Mother glanced down at me and grimaced, *A doggy with a bone, are you?*

It was just great she said that, as it gave us an excuse to let ourselves go without Gina Lucellini realising her hair-do was the main cause of our fun. All of us started laughing.

Gina's laugh might have reminded you of a soprano's vibrato, it usually came without warning and without any noticeable build up of volume, just bursting out of her only to die again as suddenly. If you'd heard her you'd 've creased up.

When we were a little older we'd occasionally spend an afternoon at the Lucellini's. Something would make us snigger, probably something so insignificant we'd hardly remember it afterwards. Her husband would join in.

Enrico Lucellini about the same height as his wife with a girth to match. His forearms heavy and hairy, his head round and all bald on top, with only a thin strip of dark fuzzy hair going from the temples to the back. Slightly bulgy brown eyes glistened with an irrepressible Italian sense of fun.

He used to refer to his hairstyle as: the Monk Cut. Sometimes he'd point up to his bald head and joke that he'd been a friar in his last life but was taking a break this time round to make children. He'd wink and bend closer to us, speaking in a mock whisper loud enough for his wife to hear and end by saying, *But don't you go telling Gina.*

Striding in from the kitchen with folded arms and a scowl over her smile, she'd begin to chase him with a huge wooden spoon. He'd run around holding his hands behind his head crying, *Help the abbess is after her poor friar!*

Enrico's laughter was as uninhibited as a schoolboy's only in bass, and could likewise come as unexpectedly as a white rabbit popping goofilly up from a magician's top hat.

When Enrico laughed everybody sort of wanted to join in. And he could interlace his chuckling with naughty undertones reminiscent of a Jasper from some Victorian melodrama about to sneak off on a spree of seduction.

As I was saying, some little something would start us off. We two might be on the floor leaning against the sofa and laughing with Enrico. Gina would throw open the kitchen door, probably holding a mixing bowl in one hand and a wooden spoon in the other. She'd stare at us curiously then break into one of her voluminous falsetto giggles.

You'd double up. And then, as her laughing suddenly let up, the power of Enrico's deep guffaw would rise. And you'd wait for her to come in again. Even though you were expecting it, even though you knew it was coming, its return still sounded unimaginatively funny.

We'd be writhing on the floor, the next laugh coming before the one before could get out, our bellies churning and vibrating. And they'd carry on. The one setting the other off on a new round of merriment. The pitch and loudness of guffaw and giggle varying almost as if they were engaged in an operatic duet, some unending Wagnerian farewell done after the manner of Gilbert and Sullivan by tone-deaf amateurs.

Tears would be streaming from us, the interactive audience. We'd dearly want out from the pain of our belly spasms but couldn't stop. I remember once vividly seeing my sister lying on her back wildly stamping her feet and wailing with a glee that wouldn't out.

Finally, or so you thought, all hilarity would settle. We two would be groaning with rib-ache and exhaustion but how glad to get release. Gina might be slumped in an armchair holding on to her mixing bowl as if it were a passionate lover. Enrico, smirking from one to the other of us, would let out a roguish chuckle. And you'd know, you'd just know Gina would join in. She always did.

And then the whole carousel could start over again.

There have been times in my life when I forgot how to laugh. Once I went a whole year without any sense of laughter inside me.

Thinking back today to such incidents of boyhood merriment when we lived through literally minutes of irrepressible fun makes me poignantly and belatedly aware that the child in me has gone missing. And that no matter how valuable adult experiences might be, a man is much, much more than his maturity.

And how long has it been now since last seeing the Lucellinis? Sometimes I imagine them together in an old people's home showing around photos of their great grandchildren. Enrico hairless except for his eyebrows, Gina with a silvery ostrich-bun but both still with that same magical sincerity in their mirth.

Maybe they were one of the reasons I always loved everything Italian.

When young Mr Lucellini like his father had been involved with the Communist Party. After the fascists took power and before the outbreak of the Second World War he and his newly wedded Gina came to the US. They'd had four children in quick succession. By the time we got to know them, all but one had fled the nest. And the youngest, a daughter, had wedding plans. One son was away at college and the two eldest children were married and living out West.

Looking back I think Gina Lucellini must have seen me and Maria as potential surrogate grandchildren. She was anyway always going on to my mother to get out and enjoy herself for she and Enrico would any time, just any time be happy to take care of us kids.

Anyway to get back to the story, after we'd stopped laughing outside the hairdressers, Mrs Lucellini carried on the conversation. Mother listened, Gina talked, her English racing along as rapidly as if it were Italian – allegrissimo. Though she'd often momentarily break off to look at us, give us a big smile and say something like, "Che bellissimi ragazzi!" or, "Che carini!" And touch our cheeks or ruffle our hair. Luckily the sun was shining from behind her so we couldn't really look up at her ostrich bun otherwise we'd never have kept our faces straight.

All at once she stopped gabbling, took mother by the arm and changed the tone of her voice, *You know what Marta*, (she always called her Marta or Martina never Martha) *You know why I've had my hair done?* Pushing it up proudly with her hand. *The Parisian plume style it's called. You know why I've had it done? It's because of the Cardinal. The Cardinal is holding Mass in the big town on Sunday morning. What do you think of that, a Prince of the Church is coming!*

When she said Prince of the Church, Maria's whole expression changed, she looked directly at me with wide eyes, took me by the sleeve and started shaking my arm wildly.

Mrs Lucellini bent down toward us, *Wouldn't you two like to come and hear the Cardinal and see a real Prince of the Church?*

We nodded excitedly.

Good, I'll get tickets for the hired bus.

Mother said something like, *But*. She just hated having to take things. It upset her to take any form of charity. But if anyone was able to give her something, I guess it was Gina Lucellini.

No buts Martina! This is my treat. I want you to do me the favour of letting me take you and the children to see the Cardinal.

Mrs Lucellini's last words were, *I'll try to get my heretic to come, who knows, perhaps the Cardinal can convert him.*

I think Enrico Lucellini took it as a kind of compliment when people called him 'the Heretic'. Though once to a group of Italian buddies outside the Church I'd heard him say as he lifted up his forefinger, *Heretic no, agnostic yes!*

Not that I had the faintest idea what agnostic meant at that time.

Mrs Lucellini waddled away with her shopping bags. Mother glanced over to her reflection in the hairdressers' window and pushed up the back of her hair. Perhaps trying to picture herself with a bird-tail bun.

Isn't Mr Lucellini an agnasty Catholic?

Eh? frowning her way back to the daily reality of being mother to two inquisitive children, *Oh, you mean agnostic. Yes Ray, he's fond of saying he's an agnostic Catholic.*

Maria looking real puzzled as she spoke, *Is that different from a Roman Catholic?*

5. Cardinal Questions

We just couldn't wait to get back home and talk about it together. Prince of the Church! Wow! We did check with mother if we'd heard right, *Is a cardinal really a prince of the church?*

Yes, cardinals are called princes of the church.

Later we got to wondering if 'are called' was quite the same as 'are'. Maria solved that one though, saying we could easily find out because princes had princesses so we just had to wait and see if the Cardinal brought his princess along with him.

We were over the moon. So much so we more or less began to take it for granted that cardinals really were princes. And this meant there was hope even for Father Rufus. He just had to be made a cardinal then being a prince he could take a princess – and all his missing-something misery could breeze over into the happily-ever-after.

It was all so simple. We only had to get him made into a cardinal.

But how?

We asked mother, *How do you become a cardinal?*

She pouted her lips for a moment, *Mm, it must be the Pope who decides who is to be a cardinal.*

Everything was falling perfectly into place! We could cut through all the difficulties and appeal directly to his Holiness in Rome!

We didn't waste time. I hunted out a scrap of paper and we sharpened our few coloured pencils so we could write to him. Maria felt pretty sure of the outcome because Father Rufus would be a good prince. Even mother thought he was great and she didn't let herself go about just anyone.

And most of all he was experienced. He'd already had one princess and lost her.

I guess we only knew about princes from fairytales. Where adventure was all about rescuing the princess and wedding her so living could be happy ever after.

After putting the pencils side by side on the coffee table we decided the red one would be the most proper. I'd only been at school a year or two and my spelling, to use my teacher's words, left much to be desired. I knelt by the coffee table with the red pencil.

Do you spell 'Pope', pe, oh, pe?

Maria twisted her nose and shrugged her shoulders. In my best handwriting I started to write. It went something like this:

"Deer Pop

Plees, plees make Farther Rufus a card in all. He has alredy lost a prinses so he nos what its like to be a prins. He is a good preest. Even mother thinks he is grate.

luv

Ray and Maria"

We even added a postscript:

"PS. Farther Rufus can run."

The letter was never sent.

After finishing it I stood up and proudly read it out to my sister. Then something puzzled me: If cardinals were princes who was the King? The answer though seemed fairly obvious, I mused it aloud, *I guess the Pope's the king of the church.*

My sister reacted – you know sometimes you could say something pretty ordinary and she'd make a qualitative jump, and put what you'd said in another, a new or a wider context.

You'd see a spider tangling with a wasp in its web and say, *Wow! that spider's having a ball with the wasp*.

And she might reply starry-eyed, *Gee, even creepy-crawlies can fall in love*.

Anyway after I'd said that about the Pope being king. I could see a rainbow of emotions stirring and contending in her. She jumped up and shouted, *He's not!* Then she grabbed a pencil and jabbed it down on the letter breaking the newly sharpened point. *He is not, you dumbum!*

But if cardinals are princes the Pope must be-

I never got to the end of the sentence. Maria overturned the coffee table and ran off. I gave a cry of pain. The table had landed on my foot.

As mother rushed in from the kitchen, my sister tripped and fell headlong into her shins. I was hopping about and wailing. Luckily the foot wasn't broken or anything. Though a nasty black and blue bruise appeared the next day.

She got us to calm down and stop crying. We were on the settee, mother in the middle.

Okay what was it all about?

I only said the Pope must-

He said, the Pope was married to Mary.

I did not!

You did! You said the Pope was king which means he must be married to the Queen. And Mary's the Queen of the Church, isn't she?

Her brown eyes were making an intense appeal to mother. I threw my head down on mother's lap and broke into tears. Maria laid herself down crying on top of me.

My mother let us cry. She didn't say anything she just put her arms round us. And she let us sob for quite a while.

Thinking back now I'd give quite a lot to see mother's expression then. With her children weeping profusely over the ecclesiastic and marital status of the Bishop of Rome.

Eventually she got us to sit up. We leant against her, her arms round us.

Now listen you two. The Pope isn't married to Mary and he isn't King of the Church. He's the vicar of Christ.

I'd heard this before. One of my school friends was Anglican not Catholic, he always called priests, vicars.

My sister didn't know the word, *What's vicar?*

It means, well, it's a stand-in, I think. You know what that means, don't you?

The kettle started boiling. She stood up, glad I'm sure to break off from ecclesiastical explanations.

As you grow up, you gradually get inklings of how intricate relationships can be within the Church Militant.

Anyway my sister was real relieved Mary wasn't betrothed to the Pope. Elation drained out of her expression though when she asked me how my foot was, I made an excruciation on my face. She reached gently down to touch my foot, the wrong foot.

I shrieked. She jumped back looking aghast.

Mother dropped something in the kitchen and came running in, *What now!*

I was just going to tell Maria, I'd have to use her for a crutch. I leaned toward my sister and whispered, *Wrong foot.*

Her shocked look went over into something else. She slapped my good foot and shoved me off the couch. I yelped, and on all fours looked up and appealed to mother.

She's hurt my other foot now as well. I'll have to ride her piggyback for the rest of the day.

Maria leapt on my back and gave my ass a thwack. *You can crawl round like a creepy, you big slug-bug!*

6. Hair an' Ticks

Very early next morning I woke up chuckling to myself. I'd just dreamed I was at some sort of solemn gathering. Standing in front of me was Mrs Lucellini, her bird-tail hair-do was as big as a full-blown ostrich in my dream. Then I noticed her husband shrunk to bug size and popping up out of his wife's hair. He winked at me and with a cheeky grin growled, *I'm a dirty hair-rat tick.*

His accompanying bass-voiced schoolboy laughter ringing through the building was my last impression from the dream.

I lay wide awake in the greyness before morning thinking back to that time over a year ago when we first got to know the Lucellinis ...

There was this one time when people were milling around in front of the church after a service, I saw someone come up and give Mr Lucellini a slap on the back saying, *Well if it isn't Enrico the Heretic.*

Later that day I asked mother about the meaning of the word as she was in the kitchen cutting up her vegetables.

What's a hair a' tick?

Hair-rat hic? She crinkled her brows, *Oh, you probably mean heretic. Well, a heretic is someone who spreads false doctrine.*

About a week before she'd read us a story of a witch who'd pretended to be a doctor but had really gone around making people fall sick with her vile potions.

Is it anything to do with witches?
Mm, yeah, something like that.

As I wandered out into the garden, I felt pretty pleased with myself for finding out that heretics went around doing wrong doctoring.

But what this all had to do with hair and ticks was still dark to me. Everything got sort of mixed up when I tried to think about it. Then, just like that, it came to me: Hair-rat-ticks must go around spreading hair-ticks!

Though just how you could catch hair-ticks from bald Enrico Lucellini was as yet an unsolved puzzle.

It wasn't every Sunday he came to church but when he did, I'd take the chance to sneak up to see if ticks or bugs were crawling about in his band of black hair. Generally Italians were boisterously babbling around him so my scouting missions weren't noticed.

Only after I'd done this a couple of times he saw me!

He pushed his chin down into his chest, tilted his head to one side and stared at me from under dark eyebrows, a smile creeping over his face.

It was a shock I can tell you to be caught by the eye of a hair a' tick.

Later that afternoon I began to wonder, what with hair an' ticks being related to witches and everything, if his chin-on-the-chest head-tilting business mightn't have been a way of putting a spell on an unsuspecting soul. So I tried practising his technique on Maria's toy duck as it sat in the armchair.

Mother gave me a curious smile as she passed by, *What are you up to?*

I'm doing magic on the duck.

You don't do magic by twisting your neck, my lad.

Then she did something which wasn't at all a typical mother-thing for her. She lowered her face down to mine squinting meanly. Suddenly as if casting a spell on me with her hands she wailed in a screechy voice, *Whaaaah! Abracadabra! Now you're a toad!*

My sister came running in, Mother said to her in that same screechy witch tone, *Look! He's an ugly toad with warts and suckers instead of fingers.*

I glanced down. My hands, thankfully, were still there. But a cry was beginning to work up inside me. I ran over and threw myself face down in the easy chair with the duck.

Mother let out a shriek. Maria was thumping her thigh with both fists.

Even then, I guess, she was pretty good at taking my part.

Next time I went scouting for ticks, he spotted me at once and gave me his chin-on-the-chest. Then holding out a bag of candies he came over. Almost as if in a dream I took one, popped it in my mouth and dashed back to mother.

The candy tasted nice but soon began to burn my tongue. It was nearly half dissolved before the thought bobbed up that it might be poisoned.

A hair a' tick way of tricking a kid into chobbling an infected humbug. I spat it out.

Too late! By the time we got home I could feel creepy crawlies all over my scalp. I'd caught ticks for sure. As soon as we got home I rushed into mother's bedroom and fearfully peered into her dressing-table mirror. There were one or two whitish specks in my hair. They weren't crawling about though, or were they? Did that one move or didn't it?

I rubbed my eyes then started rubbing my hair violently. In the midst of my scratching I noticed Maria standing near, watching me without saying a word.

It's the ticks, I can't stand them.

She went straight over grabbed the clock on the bedside table and shoved it under a pillow. Then came back to me. I was still scratching.

They're eating me away. I bent down and pushed my hair toward her. *Can you see them?*

Ray, a serious note in her voice, *I don't think you can see ticks, only hear them.*

No! Not clock ticks. Tick ticks, the biting kind!

Maria searched my hair but couldn't see any. But I wasn't convinced. Then I remembered the magnifying glass Uncle Uri had given us.

Even through the lens she couldn't detect crawlies. But maybe we needed more light. Out in the sunshine. Still no visible creepies. Mother was over on the other side of the garden plucking a lettuce.

All at once it came to me, *Maria, burn the ticks. Focus it on my head and burn the ticks, burn them, burn them!*

My hair was fairly short. In a couple of moments you could smell singeing. Then *Ow!* It was hot, I cried out in pain.

Mother rushed over.

Maria peeped shyly up at her, one eye huge behind the glass.

She was burning my ticks.

After a telling off and a stern warning never to use a magnifying glass for burning. She too thoroughly searched my scalp.

Neither ticks nor lice. Now go and wash your hands for dinner.

Running back to the house you just can't imagine how great it was to be found free of ticks. Like emerging from a dip in the lake on a scorching afternoon.

The exuberant feeling lasted till early evening when a dark cloud descended. What if the ticks hatch out at night? What if they start creeping out of me while I'm asleep?

Maria was only four, it was before I used to take her into all my secrets. But now I was scared. Surely not even mother was a match for hair a' tick magic.

On the easy chair with my sister beside me, in whispers I told her all about the poisoned humbug. She listened open mouthed while tightly holding on to one of my hands. Mother entered from the kitchen. I clammed up. She went past us into the bedroom and came straight out again, *All right where is it? What have you done with the clock?*

The hour of doom was nearing. I did everything to avoid being sent up to bed because if I fell asleep ... no, no, it was too horrifying even to think about.

In the end mother lost patience with my stalling and ordered me off to bed. My sister went up in front of me. Each stair was a big step for her. But at least she had a teddy bear. All I had was nearly hatched out ticks.

I slumped on my pillow and began sniffling, tears coming into my eyes. Maria peeped in through my doorway, shook her head sadly and left. She descended the stairs still clinging to her teddy.

Mother was kneading dough and way off in her thoughts. Maria surprised her, *I want to ask, er, to ask about him. Him with the topless hair.*

Mother frowned.

You know him! Him! You know.

Mother shook her head with a smile.

Him! My sister was making as if to cut off her locks, *Him with the sweaty head.*

Mother looked at her blankly.

You know him, you do know, my sister was getting herself worked up, she threw the bear down and stamped.

I don't.

You do!

I do not, little Missy!

You do! Him, the hairy tick.

It dawned on mother, *Oh you mean Mr Lucellini. He isn't a heretic, it's just that he isn't quite sure if he really believes.*

Not a hairy tick! Maria started dancing around with excitement, *Then Ray can't get ticks from the candy!*

She picked up the bear and did a twirl with it.

What's all this about ticks, young lady?

Maria stopped her motion and hung her head. I'd given her strict instructions not to tell.

What's Ray up to?

He's crying.

Is he afraid he's caught something from that boiled sweet Mr Lucellini gave him, ticks perhaps?

Still with hanging head, she half nodded.

Mother was washing her hands and suppressing a big grin, *Let's go up and comfort him.*

After Maria left I began to wonder if I ought to pray. While thinking about making a prayer, the story mother read us earlier that day came into my mind. It was about a prince who had to follow a path through a dark wood where scrapings and screeching could be heard. He'd had to overcome his fear of bats and ... and here was I sniffling just because of ... suddenly I got mad, real mad at the ticks.

I'd get them. I jumped up, seized one of my shoes and sat up in bed pulling a blanket round me, the shoe held up firmly in my right hand.

I wasn't going to sleep. No! I'd stay awake. All night if need be and if any ticks dared poke their gluttonous snouts up from my scalp then bam! Bam! Bam!

Mother came into my room, *Ray what, what are you doing, why are you holding your shoe up?*

It's to bash the ticks.

What a lousy thing, real lousy, when your own mother responds to your secret fears with a bellyful of laughter.

7. X-Plosives

At our church there were lots of Italians, some Poles and Ukrainians, a few Irish people (though the Irish contingent lived a long way off from us) and one British couple: the Hemmings. Their only son had found a well paid job in the States and emigrated. After reaching retirement they came over here and stayed about a year in a house half a mile or so away from ours. They didn't speak English English. They were from Gornal in the Black Country in England. When I heard the name Black Country I asked mother if the people there were black. She cast back her hair, her eyes shining and told me in the old days there were so many factories and furnaces and big, big chimneys that they called the region the Black Country. She stood on tiptoes, arms held high as she said, *Chimneys belching out thick black smoke and soot*, while moving her hands to imitate smoke and lowering her voice half an octave.

Later I heard the Black Country was the cradle of the Industrial Revolution.

The Black Country, wow! I pictured all the grass covered in soot and people feeling their way forward through smoggy mists with arms stretched out in front of them.

The Hemmings never said people or persons, they said folk. And used chaps and wenches instead of boys and girls. So Maria was a little wench, me a little chap. They spoke the most outlandish language imaginable. I sort of figured it must be because all that industrial fog made them hoarse so their voices came from right down in their boots. You'd probably have to visit Iceland or Finland or even Siberia to find the like of that elemental power in their speaking. They'd compress a word in their speech organs as you might a snowball in your hands then launch it forcefully from deeper tone registers. The vowels were short and chiselled like stone or else so expansive they'd last thrice the length of ordinary English ones. And the consonants, well, plosives weren't common or garden stop sounds they were 'X-plosives' spoken with a vigour to knock you back against the wall. A real worker's dialect in total contrast to snobbish lah-di-dah posh upper-class English English.

Take the word 'half'. They'd clip off the initial 'h' and say aaahf' with stress and length on the vowel, and an intonation going down then up and a 'h' inserted after the vowel to give extra thrust to the 'f'. There was more gumption in one of their short words than a whole sentence of sophisticated English.

And they spoke loud, compared to them Americans are a nation of whisperers.

Bill and Ann Hemmings used to bring bottles of beer and stout when they visited. Once Bill had just sunk his beer and was about to wipe off a foam moustache when I asked him if they spoke like they did so they could throw words to each other through the thick Gornal smog.

E day arf loff (literal translation: he didn't half laugh, i.e. he really laughed). And then he told me it was, *Cus a th'owd Anglo-Saxon* (because of the old Anglo-Saxon).

Owd Anglo Saxon – that sounded pretty scary, not the kind of thing a six year old wanted to hear about before going upstairs to sleep in his own room by himself in a little house in a clearing in the woods.

They could change over to speaking a slightly funny version of the Queen's English. But as mother loved language she always encouraged 'em t' spake owd Gornal (encouraged them to speak the old Gornal dialect).

And my sister, she'd just sit entranced on the floor looking up silently while imitating their speech with movements of her mouth.

Sometimes me and Maria used to play 'spakin-owd-Gornal' together. It's probably pretty hard for Americans to realise just how different their language was. The Gornal folk'd growl, 'Aaah bay', going down in tone on that long 'ah' then shooting up with a barely perceptible pause before 'b' and the 'hay' exploded across the room. When they just wanted to say, 'I'm not'.

They'd roar, "Jome mekkin' er ghu saft, jo bin!" Instead of saying: you're making her go crazy, you are.

Or, "Jo bay duin that, bin ya, owd mon?" Instead of 'you aren't doing that, are you dear?'

I'm pretty sure they never needed street fights in Gornal as their dialect was alive with its own verbal fisticuffs.

Maybe by now television's mundane uniformity has sucked much of the life from Black Country dialects. But looking back today a genuine sense of gratitude arises in me for the privilege of being able to listen to Bill and Ann Hemmings speak their elemental Anglo-Saxon-resounding Gornal English.

How many influences combined to nurture language in me? My mother's Irish deep in my childhood and always in our home.

My father's Russian and his gruff American deeper than the child in me recalls.

The plethora of accents (and languages) around church and in school, all under the dominance of the Fifties' Zeitgeist in America.

The King James' Bible. Fairytales in un-American words and worlds. (Sometimes I think McCarthy's mother never whispered to him, "Once upon a time ...") Arthurian tales, Tolkien, Shakespeare, what we read came mostly from Britain, not from the deadened competence and sub-clause of Southern Middle-Class English suburbia but from that language spoken, or once spoken, in the hearts of the British Folk.

American English was always a second dialect.

Yet my first? I don't know, my English has no land-based or community-registered home.

Many of my closest friends have been from other parts of the globe. Much of my adult life has been in Europe.

And all the journalistic writing, I've done, often under pseudonyms, sometimes I think I've lived, time-wise if not space-wise, in a menagerie of dialect. I put on or change styles to write or speak as a fashion-conscious lady chooses her dresses or casts them off.

Yet I have loved that indefatigable yet unintrusive Spirit of the English language. How strong she is to survive 'simple' English, bureaucratic and legalistic strains, the barbarism of much academic discourse, and the media's shameless plugging of the Market and the cliché. How selfless she is to give herself to manifold non-native English dialects and to live not only in one country or territory but among many nations all around the globe.

How I should have loved to have beheld her with eyes open to her spirit in the flush and freedom of her Shakespearean youth.

8. Sheepish

Why have I been going on about the Hemmings? Well, through them the problem of Mr Lucellini's baldness was solved.

At least I thought it was.

Referring to a man who was going pretty thin on top, Ann Hemmings touched mother's arm and said, *An iz az boorld az a ewe-tick* (meaning: 'and he's as bald as a ewe tick').

That was it! That was it! The you-ticks must have gobbled up Mr Lucellini's hair!

By then I'd sort of gotten to realise he wasn't a dangerous species of hair a' tick. It even seemed a shame he'd caught ticks and had his hair gorged, right down to the roots. So when the next service he attended was over and we'd left the church I went up to him. And as he gave me his usual chin-on-the-chest greeting as I asked shyly if ticks had eaten all of his hair.

His eyes opened wider as he stooped down to me, his jaw turning to one side, *What did you say?*

Have they, have the ticks eaten your hair?

With a wild smack on his knee he well nigh doubled up laughing. This sudden reaction startled me. I scampered off, heart thumping, tears welling in my eyes. When I got to mother and turned back I could see the Italians shouting and threshing their arms about in the air. Mrs Lucellini left the group and walked toward us. I hid in my mother's skirts.

After exchanging a greeting with mother she bent done to me, *Poverino!* And tried to explain that he hadn't meant to frighten me, it was just his Friar-Tuck way of laughing.

She pointed over to her husband. *I'll shoot him*, she said and sent an imaginary arrow whizzing from an imaginary bow, it got him in the lower gut.

He lurched about as though on his last legs. Maria was hopping about excitedly while I still clung to mother's clothes.

Not many days after this I asked mother what they did with heretics. She was washing up and gazing out of the window, and just answered, *Oh, they used to burn them*.

I must have looked stricken because she quickly assured me they didn't do that any more. Burnings only happened in olden times, in the Middle Ages. And she added, *Nowadays we don't deal so harshly with heretics*.

I slouched out of the house thinking it was really mean that someone should be burned for a spot of tick-spreading. I knew tick-spreading wasn't a nice thing to do and maybe them ol' hair a' ticks should have got a thrashing or something but to be roasted alive over a log fire – that sounded real mean, not fair somehow.

Sort of staring around the garden and questioning myself, if nowadays hair a' ticks aren't treated harshly (and I wasn't quite sure what 'harshly' meant) what did happen to them?

Perhaps only their books and things get tossed on the fire or maybe – a picture of Mr Lucellini sitting on a bench outside the church sprang into my mind. I'd noticed there was a reddish patch on his bald top. Though sometimes it looked white. It could have been a scar.

A scar! Perhaps that's what not harshly meant. Nowadays they don't burn the man, they burn the ticks. Only sometimes the hair goes up in smoke as well. Involuntarily I found myself thinking what might happen if I caught ticks and if fire was set to them. Peering into an imaginary mirror I saw myself with only a thin band of hair like Mr Lucellini and a big red blotch on my smouldering bald top. I wanted to yell out: It wasn't my fault the ticks got to me!

Life became easier when Maria was bit older because I took her into confidence about most everything. And we didn't get so tied up in knots by all those insoluble problems grown-ups strew around to mesmerise us kids with. Well, not that often. But just then all I wanted to know was what had happened to Mr Lucellini's hair. Perhaps deep down I was scared about what might happen to mine one day, or maybe I just felt sorry for him.

Anyway next Sunday in church before Mass I couldn't sit still, I kept turning round to see if he'd duck up. Mrs Lucellini entered and went toward the holy water. Then her husband shoved back the door and I was away and put myself in front of him before he reached the water.

Did they burn your hair?

His chin began to turn down, his head tilted I wasn't sure if he'd properly heard me so I repeated the question in earnest. *Did they really burn off your hair?*

For a couple of seconds he seemed to be tuning in to my question, his eyes bulged, his jaw started to tremble and then, well, how should I say. Mm, it was probably a good thing back there in the days of Robin Hood that the trees in Sherwood Forest had thick foliage to deaden sounds if Friar Tuck's laughter was anything like Mr Lucellini's.

His wife reacted like a hound dog to the disturbance, pushing almost kicking her husband out of the church.

Before the heavy door swung to I heard him being pummelled black and blue in abusive Italian.

Mother took hold of my arm and forcibly brought me back to our pew.

When Mr Lucellini came back in he had a long sheepish face on, his head bowed. But when he caught sight of me he winked.

9. A Singing Piccolo

My mother was blessed with a clear and beautiful soprano. Shortly after getting married she'd taken a few singing lessons and found she could reach the high B and C.

If you hadn't known my sister and if you'd met her when she was two or three years old and if you hadn't realised she was so young then you might have been tempted to think she was doing some kind of deliberate falsetto. As she grew older those up-in-the-clouds tones descended somewhat. Her voice was still high pitched but not such as would make people turn their heads in the street if she spoke.

One time mother tried to see just how far up Maria's voice could go. She began a song on the C below the Soprano's top C. I could just about reach that but they could easily go on up the scale. Mother wistfully sucking her teeth and looking askance at my sister, plonked a note on the piano and started the same song on G below the Soprano's very highest notes. Mother just about managed to get to the C above it. Maria went higher effortlessly.

Whoa, Whoa! Mother stopped her, *I don't believe it, you're a singing piccolo.*

That singing piccolo sounded hilarious. I used to tease her with the nickname for quite a while after. Not that I knew what a piccolo was, not till mother explained it was a flute-like instrument so high pitched that even when the whole orchestra was banging away at full blast you could still hear its trills.

Mother gave us special attention in church, well because of Maria, I guess, her voice being not only high but so clear and carrying that even if she spoke normally in there then all the congregation could hear us, hear her I mean. And mother hated us bringing attention on ourselves. So she always made us be quiet in church. We wouldn't talk and if we really had to it would be in whispers. We never felt though as if we were being forced to bow to some rule or other, it just became habit. And anyway both of us learnt to love the quietness in our little church.

As I said when Maria came to be about four or five those other worldly tones in her voice settled down. She still had a very high pitched voice but it sounded more natural. Excepting when she got excited. Then the decibel level of her voice would rise and her register jump up an octave or so.

10. Breathless

The day of the Cardinal's Mass arrived. We'd had trouble sleeping the night before. We'd been whispering in bed together about the Prince. About whether he would ride to the Mass on horseback, whether he would be fair with blue eyes or tall and dark, and whether his princess would be dressed in silver or white.

Mother got up early because we had first to walk to our church to get the coach and then had a longish journey to the big town. We came early, well before the hired bus arrived. Mother always got us to be early for just about everything.

People started arriving. Then the bus chunted in. Passengers leisurely ascended. Soon we were the only three left standing outside. The driver started the engine and told mother he'd have to leave if they were to make it on time.

The Lucellinis were late. They were always late.

Just then we heard a shout, Gina and her husband came scurrying toward the bus. As she came closer I could see that she'd somehow managed to keep her ostrich-butt hairdo more or less intact. Apparently she'd used hair lacquer liberally and slept in some kind of gigantic reinforced hair net.

Mother bundled us onto the bus, me and my sister shared a seat next to her. Coaches in the late Fifties were pretty humperty-bumperty. They really shook you up especially when waiting at road junctions. The weather was miserable, overcast. I could have done with an extra hour in bed and an early lunch.

Have you ever had the feeling you're gonna be let down, everything seems to be going along fine, you're on the way to something really exciting, you should be over the moon but, but somehow a let-down sensation starts to deflate you even before even get there. Something like this took a grip on me as we drove along.

We hardly ever travelled on buses. Mother was worried in case Maria got sick. So she sat my sister on her lap. Maria snuggled up and closed her eyes. Maybe she was off to dreamland, wonderland or sleep. I felt all alone and very tiny on my seat. I had to stretch to see properly out of the window, but it seemed too much effort so I just stared bleakly up at the grey sky.

The Lucellinis were sitting just in front of us and babbling away in Italian. I started kicking the back of their seat. Mother told me to stop and added, *Try thinking something nice instead of fidgeting.*

I tried to picture a prince on horseback but only felt the bus juddering under me and saw drops of water rolling down the panes after it began to rain.

Maria seemed fast asleep. She spent the whole ride on mother's lap.

On the last part of the ride when we reached the city I switched places with Mrs Lucellini. Kneeling on the window seat while her husband leaned over and pointed out people in the street and places of interest.

Just as the bus slowed down to pull in to the cathedral car park we noticed someone opening up a mobile hamburger stand. Hamburgers! I could almost smell them. I'd only had a cup of herb tea and a tiny crust of bread. Mother had taken just a glass of water. Maria hardly touched a thing.

Mr Lucellini spoke my thought aloud, *Hamburgers!* He repeated the word with longing and looked down at his pot belly with a little-boy-lost expression, *Water, Gina said only water.*

I guess his wife hadn't let him eat breakfast because of communion.

As we climbed off the bus I heard a strange gurgling sound and turning back saw Mr Lucellini pat his midriff.

My rumble tum, he moaned with a pouting face.

The belly groan repeated itself with double decibels.

Mother carried my sister in her arms. Mrs Lucellini walked alongside chuntering. I followed miserably. Her husband was sucking his teeth and seemed preoccupied as he strolled beside me.

The two women sat down on a bench by the cathedral building. Still on mother's lap Maria stretched her arms then her legs, made a 'mm' sound and cuddled up again to mother. Then she squinted over at me and called me. When I went over she put her arms round my neck and gave me a squeeze, whispering in my ear, *Now we'll soon see the Prince!* Her face, glad and expectant, had a sort of been-wandering-in-fairyland look about it.

Trying my best to forget the melancholy bus trip and get myself in the mood, I assented, *Yes, the prince,* but my voice sounded flat. I tried to straighten up but she made a renewed grab at my neck and clung on nearly causing me to lose balance and tumble onto them.

Mother took us both by the wrists and scrutinised our appearances, she smiled, *Aren't either of you two going to have a wee before the service?*

We shook our heads. I began wondering if a real prince needed to dismount or whether he could relieve himself while riding in the saddle. Then it crossed my mind that the cardinal might come on a white horse and if he did so, would he canter into the church or tie it up outside?

There were no horses to be seen as yet.

Mother's question must have elicited a response in Mrs Lucellini for she hurried off to the ladies. Her husband gave a satisfied grunt and curled his lips roguishly as he observed her walk away. He had her huge handbag in one hand and a box in the other. He put them on the bench beside mother and asked her if she could look after them while he paid a visit.

Just as he turned to walk away, an Italian buddy of his put a hand on his shoulder and started off twenty to the dozen. Enrico didn't appear too captivated by what he was being told because he kept casting impatient glances in the direction of the toilets. When the guy showed no sign of letting up he started crossing his legs, doubling up and making obvious gestures. His comrade grinned as Enrico hobbled off towards the lavatories.

He only got halfway though then straightened up, looked furtively about him and doubled back making a wide arc toward the gates. There were plenty of people milling around in the car park by then so I only caught a couple of glimpses of him but I did see him go out through the gates. It seemed a funny sort of thing to do, maybe there'd been a queue or something.

Just then I heard Mrs Lucellini's voice behind me, *Now Martina, let me show you what's in the box*. The box was big. As she opened it, I had my nose right over the packing paper inside. She pulled out a straw hat and triumphantly held it up, *Eccolo!* It had blue and yellow artificial flowers stuck on it and a long pink feather sticking up from the back and curling up and over the front brim in an arc.

What do you think Marta? Gina was beaming, *Haven't shown it to Enrico yet, it's a surprise.*

She lifted it higher and set it carefully on her, well, you wouldn't so much say head as on her hair. You saw her face then above this the upward backward sweep of her lacquered hair and then on top of her ostrich hair-do rested the straw hat. Its centre in a vertical line up from the back of her head, the feather arching forward to finish a little above her forehead. She gave the tip of the feather a flick with her finger as she spoke, *The man in the shop said it was genuine flamingo.*

Imagine if some mischievous spirit had captured the concentrated essence of all those times when you've ever broken into unstoppable laughter, distilled it into liquid and injected it into your abdomen.

Something like this was shaking in my gut as I watched Gina put the hat on. I staggered behind mother opened my mouth wide and bit ... into her behind. She shrieked and swivelled round. The look she gave me was one of wildness mingled with merriment, an Irish note in her exclamation, *I think I've bred a bulldog!*

How she could really get it just right sometimes, my mother, a piece of pure Irish blarney. The perfect excuse to let yourself go. Gina also burst into her vibratos.

I'm not quite sure how all this might have gone on had not Maria suddenly appeared on the scene. She'd been dodging in and out between people and came running up to us. Only instead of stopping she just kind of ran smack into me.

My body was in the grip of the giggles and helpless, her impact knocked the wind right out of me. I went down sock on my bottom, making croaking noises and clawing for air. By the time I eventually got back to breathing I'd even stopped minding about Gina's hat.

Mother was adjusting the hat on Gina's lacquered plumes.

Where's my Enrico?

Oh, he went to relieve himself, said mother as she stuck a giant hair pin through the straw into the ostrich butt.

He went ... I motioned toward the toilets then swept my arm in a wide circle till it pointed to the main gateway, *that a way.*

Mrs Lucellini wrinkled her brows, *Did he go out of the gates?*

I nodded but judging from her expression I began to wonder if it mightn't have been telling on him.

Maria had run off again. Mother went to find her. Gina, with a knowing wink, took me by the arm, *Come on let's go and surprise him, Ray.*

11. Doggies

We saw him a few yards down from the Cathedral gateway sitting on a bench and holding a huge and as yet untasted hot dog. Eyeing it with such attentive loving tenderness, he didn't even notice our approach. He drew it along under his nose as you might a fat Havana cigar, sniffing so closely that a little blob of bright yellow mustard stuck to the tip of his nose. He nonchalantly brushed it away with the back of his hand as we stole towards him.

Mrs Lucellini standing by the bench legs apart, hands on hips just as the virgin fast food was raised slowly to his gaping jaws. He had just stuffed it deep between his teeth when Gina growled, *Mmmmmh!*

We caught him red-mouthed! Ketchup oozing over his jowls. He shot up. His eyes opening wide, hands dropping down by his sides. The hot dog still sticking out of his mouth. Gina Lucellini, her forefinger aloft, was winding herself up to sock him one bitch of a Neapolitan telling-off when the hot-dog broke off at his mouth and fell plosh on the sidewalk, red ketchup and yellow mustard mingling on the frankfurter.

Her finger changed to a clenched fist. She sucked in a sharp breath between her teeth and was about to turn herself loose on him when I noticed his head tilting.

He'd caught sight of the straw hat perched on the ostrich bun. One eye following the curve of the feather, his other moving off in a different line of sight, his cheeks bulging ...

I'd learnt just what that kind of expression meant. His mouth exploded.

Soggy bread, unchewed sausage, orangey red mustard mixed with ketchup just spewed out over us. Mrs Lucellini screamed. Her husband, who was making noises worthy of a walrus, sank to his knees. Choking fits spluttered between guttural belly chuckles as he crawled around like an animal.

Gina more concerned about his condition than her dress was patting him affectionately when a newcomer arrived on the scene. In a shabby raincoat, his glasses askew, middle-aged and intoxicated, with an expression possibly indicative of double vision, he came staggering toward us.

At this point Enrico's face was less than a foot above the main portion of the hot-dog. His wife seemed to be tickling him behind the ear.

The drunk's head drooped almost to his shoulder as he bent sideways to look down at Enrico's fast food remains and burped, *Do they feed dogs hamburgers nowadays?*

Something must have seemed amiss to him though because having said this he peered closer, making an unsuccessful attempt to straighten his glasses.

I'll be darned! I thought they only shaved poodles.

He tried to straighten up, his mouth opened as he caught sight of Gina's hat. He seemed to be going cross-eyed as first his nose and then his torso began to follow the hypnotic wave of the pink feather in the breeze.

Tell me Mam, is your animal a pure-bred?

Enrico responded with walrus noises. Our new acquaintance let out a gasp of alarm and half ran, half stumbled off the kerb and with a cry of, *Mad dog!* And fell full length out into the street.

Just as a flashy limousine was cruising toward us. Brakes screeched as it swerved and skidded across the road coming to a halt with its hood pointing over to the opposite sidewalk.

Luckily the road was wide and there were no parked cars, nor following or oncoming traffic.

Two young men with dark greasy hair and slick black suits jumped out of the automobile shouting angrily in Italian. Seeing this today, I'd have guessed straight away that they were members of the mob. Enrico told me later their limo had New York number plates.

Without a second's hesitation Gina Lucellini went waddling over like a gun slinger. A heated exchange in Italian followed. Which afterwards I learnt went something to this effect.

Pointing back toward us she was telling them the drunk had thought her husband was possessed by rabies. To illustrate her explanations she made biting gestures and growled. All the while her feather fluttered in the wind.

Enrico still on all fours, his head hung over what must have looked like vomit, the misuser of alcohol stretched out and moaning, and me, a little kid, standing wretchedly between them.

To be met by a woman wearing a pink plume on a straw hat stuck on top of an ostrich-butt hair-do, whose dress was splattered in fast food, whose husband was grovelling under an attack of hydrophobia, and who was bawling back at them like a Neapolitan maternal aunt was all too much for the mobsters.

Anyway by then a venerable looking priest in black had appeared in the cathedral gateway. He called over to them in good-natured Italian.

What he'd said was that if they wished to attend Holy Mass there was plenty of parking space round the side of the cathedral.

Nodding sort of respectfully to the priest the two Frankies turned their backs in disgust on Gina, got in their automobile and slammed the doors. Their limo shot out in reverse almost running her down. She shrieked, stepped backwards and tumbled just as the car backfired with a bang like a six shooter and then sped off.

Enrico must have thought they'd gunned her down. Crying out her name wildly he moved off like a sprinter. Unfortunately our friend under the influence was just scrambling to his feet, Enrico took him out like a grizzly guard might a quarterback – or a mad dog a tempting buttock.

12. Domestic Choices

The Lucellinis were a little ahead of me as we walked back to the cathedral entrance. I felt trembly and on the point of bursting into tears. Gina glanced round at me. To hide my expression I rubbed my face with my sleeve, and managed to smudge ketchup on my eyebrow.

Caro mio! She knelt on one knee in front of me as she spoke and grabbing the newly-ironed white handkerchief from Enrico's breast pocket wiped off the red smear and dried my eyes. Her kindly attention left me feeling I had to hold out and forego having a good cry just then.

Back inside the Cathedral grounds Mrs Lucellini on her husband's arm lamented the mustard blotches on my jacket. Her own dress was splattered.

She needn't have worried about me though. My mother still too keenly remembered her nights shivering in the orphanage to risk letting her own children suffer the cold. She had extra pullovers with her. I put mine on while Enrico stuffed my ketchup stained coat into a carrier bag he'd taken from Gina's enormous handbag. Then with a flourish he pulled out another dress from the handbag and triumphantly offered it to his wife. What had apparently happened was …

The night before Gina had got Enrico to look at her in dress after dress. She'd sighed over the tight fit of one, the skirt length of another, the colour of a third. In the end it came down to a choice between two. Having tried these on about half a dozen times apiece she still couldn't come to a final decision.

Scrutinising herself in the mirror, *Do you think it makes me look overweight?*

Enrico was wise enough not to answer.

Do you think pink spots are appropriate for High Mass?

He responded with a deliciously ambiguous Italianate shrug of the shoulders and twist of face.

Suddenly remembering the dress hanging up to dry, she rushed out and came back holding it up to her neck, *What do you think, perfect eh?*

Enrico seizing at once on the chance to round off the agonizations, *Yes! Yeah, yeah, as you say dear, just as you say.*

Perfect?

Perfect, as you say.

(Excuse my literal translation of their Italian.)

Those comfortably turbulent years with Gina had taught Enrico it was never a question of taking decisions for her but of making her make a decision. Or at least of making her think she'd made the decision herself. Otherwise you might have to put up with being moaned at all next day if she'd somehow gotten it into her head you'd decided for her. Not to mention how she could suddenly start going on about something you'd supposedly got into weeks, months or even years after the events themselves.

Her brow was beginning to furrow. He glanced over at the clock on the mantelpiece. The small hours were ticking away. With a sinking feeling he noticed her looking again at the other two dresses. He moved quickly over to her, put his arm round her and lifted the hem of the dress she was holding with his other hand. With a well satisfied expression he began to nod affirmatively, *Just as you said yourself dear, perfect.*

Her frown relaxed. She gave him a big smile and rubbed the stubble on his cheek with the back of her finger.

Enrico, aren't you all excited about seeing the Cardinal tomorrow?

He returned a polite, non-committal grunt.

Avoiding unnecessary marital disharmony had endowed Enrico with a mastery of the subtleties of equivocation that might have required years to mature through Scholastic or Jesuit training.

They walked in stately fashion to their boudoir, Gina's left arm, around his waist, his right arm around her shoulder, while their free arms held the perfect dress in front of them as if it were a costly stole.

From the bathroom sounds of hairspray. It took a lot to keep ostrich ends in place. She entered the bedroom with her giant hairnet on. The smell of hair lacquer hung heavy around her. Enrico felt a sense of suffocation as she lay down beside him. He was convinced continual inhalation of his wife's spray since her change of hairstyle had caused him to develop allergies to almost any kind of paint, perfume or lacquer.

On her belly beside him, she gave a contented mm-sound and twisted slightly. The hairnet tickled his nose. He straightened up coughing almost uncontrollably.

Enrico, how hysterical!

When the coughing fit went off, he lay down again with his face turned away from his wife and her hairnet. Overtired and prone to snore he got a shove from his spouse whenever decibels vibrated with his breathing.

When his daytime senses finally drowsed off, dreams came, at first in very disordered patterns then they became far from pleasant ...

(Much later Enrico told us about the wild sequence of dreams he had that night. In fact he entertained us with them on a number of occasions so I can still remember certain details. When I tried to put this on paper so many years later, it blew up into a short story in its own right. And maybe a lot of what I put in results from my own imagination rather than his narration. So I've left it as an appendix.
Even if what I wrote doesn't bear so much resemblance to what he actually dreamt, the Enrico who appears in this story captures something of the Enrico I knew and loved.)

When he finally awoke, he felt an unbearable weight pressing on is chest. His wife was lying across him in her gigantic hairnet. The hairnet was causing was nostrils to itch.
Enrico's nights were at least as adventurous as his days.

The Lucellinis were the kind of couple who even if they got up early still only managed to get out of the door after the last minute had gone by.
Their ice-cream parlour almost never opened on time.
They were only a little behind that morning. And Gina was leaving it to the very last before putting on the perfect dress so as to cut down the chance of anything getting spilt over it. It was the kind of dress you had to pull over your head.

The time when they should have strolled from their door had arrived – and passed. Gina was in the bedroom trying to get the dress on. Enrico sat in the kitchen casting a look of longing at the coffee machine.

Gina came rushing into the kitchen, her arms held up high, hands sticking out of the shortish sleeves, the dress folding over her face, its hem a little above her waist. She was desperately shouting, *Enrico, Enrico, help me, help me!*

It was the kind of dress you had to pull over your head. There was just no way it would slip over her ostrich hair-do. As he tried to pull it down she began shrieking, *No, no, my hair! Without force! No violence! Gently Enrico please gently!* She was wriggling and almost lost her balance and knocked over a chair. Her fingers were sticking up out of the sleeves and doing a good imitation of a duck's quacking bill or a gossip's tongue.

Her husband tugged the dress this way and that with his wife letting out cries at every pull. The yelling got more and more hysterical.

There was just no way the dress would slip over her hair.

So it had after all to be one of these other two. They'd been left lying around and to Gina's keen eye needed ironing. And which one to wear?

Gina took out her iron and plugged it in. Enrico put a hand to his bald-top and pointed at the clock. She looked sorrowfully back at him.

I'll have to try it on again ... but which one?
Enrico squinted and picked one up, *This.*
This?
He nodded approvingly.

While his wife struggled with it, he neatly folded the other dress, popped it into her giant handbag, pulled out the plug for the iron and grabbed his coat.

How do you like me in it? She'd almost managed to get the dress on.

Enrico was in the doorway waving, *I'm on my way. You'll never make the bus, Gina dear, it's not possible, it's unfortunate dear, most unfortunate but-*, he shrugged his shoulders and heaved a deep sigh, *I'm going, ciao, but never mind*, he gave her a big smile, *I'll pass your greetings and apologies on to the Cardinal.*

He turned and left. Gina cried out as though wounded and ran after him She got halfway down the path then rushed back in to change her shoes, and take a coat and her handbag.

Enrico waited arms folded at the garden gate. She trotted up to him, her Italian as rapid as her heartbeat.

They'd gone about twenty paces down the street when she put her hand to her mouth, dropped the handbag and hurried back in again. A certain box had been forgotten.

The coach driver was just telling mother he'd have to pull out when the Lucellinis arrived panting.

13. Of Not Being a Child

Whispering together by candlelight in our home snug within the forest, last evening like Maria I'd experienced an inner expectancy for the Prince.

Being woken early from dreamland was a trial.

Dawn's twilit linger, the warmth from our kitchen's wood-fired stove, my sister's nearness, all helped rekindle the presence of adventure.

Dewy grass, morning woodland scents and sounds, earth underfoot, a child's joy in movement.

Then the coach trip. In spite of a jolting bus journey, even in spite of seeing Gina in her hat, somehow fairytale still echoed within me.

But then my sister ran into me knocking my wind out into thin air.

An abrupt and bone-hard expulsion from fun; a momentary rearing of death's conscious inability to breathe; a premature, non-conceptual and fleeting emergence of what not to be a child means.

Then leaving the cathedral grounds to witness the Lucellinis' hot-dog shenanigans and the mobsters' skidding arrival on the scene. I'd been a barely noticed kid but had taken it all in as surely as turf might the imprint of a horse's hoof. There'd been no time to respond. Not even when Enrico was bow-wowing on all fours nor when Gina played Indian brave to Mafiosi cowboy baddies.

Shorn of dream and taking hesitant steps back toward the gates I sort of woke up to where I was. And what was I? Only a little kid in the sharp and naked daylight of late Fifties' America.

Fairytale a world away. (Its only emissary a child's innate wish to cry away all insignificance.)

As we came back in through the gates to the space in front of the cathedral, part of me wanted to hold back the big cry inside me and run to my sister to tell her that meeting the Prince Cardinal would for sure pass without magic.

And that Father Rufus might never find his princess.

14. Dyed Pink

When I saw my sister skipping around outside the Cathedral something about her told me she still waited with wonder for the Prince. I couldn't seem to speak to her, I didn't know how. Our moods were apart. If we'd been on a mountainside, she'd drifted upwards with the mists, I'd slid down on an avalanche.

Mother was saying we needed to go in and find a place before the church became too peopled. Gina marched off to change her dress. Maria ran up, gave me a big hug and raced off again. When Mrs Lucellini returned, mother took us two by either hand and all five moved toward the entrance, Enrico in the rear, Gina almost sandwiching me between her and mother, *Marta, I think this dress matches the flamingo feather best of all. Pity about being creased.*

My sister let go of mother's hand and slipped away. Gina went after her. I tugged my mother's sleeve, *Is it really from a flamingo?*

She stooped and whispered, *It's probably from a goose.*

Gina with her hands clasping Maria's arms from behind guided her back to us and said something about how good it was that so many people were coming to hear the Cardinal. Her husband put his hand on my shoulder and stopped me. The two women with my sister wedged between them began to ascend the steps. He puffed out his cheeks then sucked them in between his teeth. A real Enrico smirk transforming his face as he tapped the side of his nose and under his breath said, *A pink-dyed turkey feather!*

15. An Episode in the Cathedral

The architecture something like a Nineteenth Century American remark of a Medieval cathedral. Stained glass, dim lighting, traces of incense, the nave long and arching high above. We moved forward, tiny figures inside the church's solemnity.

The atmosphere helped settle us. Mother found a place to sit on the left near the middle and just next to the aisle. The Lucellinis sat down in front of us. People were filling the church.

Somehow in spite of all that had happened Maria's flame of expectancy was beginning to sneak into me again. We tried to be still but couldn't help casting impatient glances over our shoulders. After we were told to stop our fidgeting, my sister climbed up and knelt on her seat so she could get to see the arrival of the Prince. I was about to join her when mother told us to sit down and stop bringing attention on ourselves. Mrs Lucellini leaned back and whispered that if we wanted to see the Cardinal's entrance we could stand in the aisle.

We didn't need prompting twice!

No more people were coming in no one was moving around, no one speaking. If somebody had dropped a dime at the back of the church you'd have heard it tinkle clearly up at the altar.

When you're young it isn't always easy to put words to feelings. As I stood under the high vaulted roof, my mother and childhood pastimes somehow behind me, the cathedral more external than expectant – then what had been bubbling inside me expired into the building's congregated and stony gloom.

If you were attentive in our own little church, a magical sanctity was alive. Through a child's eyes it might have seemed as natural to see a Grail knight kneeling there before the wooden crucifix as a priest in the pulpit.

But this cathedral was full of grown ups.

One time I remember Father Rufus asking us to imagine how angels might feel while waiting for Holy Mass to begin. Here in the cathedral I had no words to tell of how holiness felt so far away and how I felt myself so little and lonely in this building full of persons and empty of angels, a mass of people waiting for a people's Mass, nameless grown-ups who didn't share, didn't even know about our adventure.

No words only mute poignancy witnessed for fairytale in the Ecclesia.

The remnant of that earlier boundless sense of expectancy had sighed from me as air from a punctured rubber ball under the boot of a passer-by.

I wanted to ask Maria if she, if she still believed a real fairytale Prince of the Church would appear or ...

Yet when I glanced down at her, she was radiant. An inner fervour shone through her giving grace to her slight movements. If I'd been cooped here with people she must have waited with those with wings.

She clasped my arm, shining depths looking at me through her brown eyes. Her voice free, clear and carrying as always, jumped up half an octave in her excitement and came out very loud, *Do you think the Cardinal will bring-*, she made a slight pause and then with renewed emphasis let out the words, *His Princess with him?*

To say everyone in the church heard her was an understatement. Her words seemed to linger within the walls. Silence held one long and pregnant moment ... until merry-monk laughter burst out of Enrico Lucellini as he swayed almost tottered into the aisle.

One person then another and another began to snigger. Suppressed tittering went around the church.

Keeping back the giggles makes them as catching as mumps. And you know how it is, the more people try to hold laughter inside in such formal get togethers the more it shakes them up.

Gina Lucellini saved the situation. She grabbed, shook, shoved her husband then rammed her straw hat down over his head as he sank to the floor. Artificial petals showered around, the long pink plume flew up and looped the loop before settling in the centre of the nave. Torrential Italian rained over him as he sat grinning in the middle of the aisle with the straw hat on his head.

This little episode gave everyone the excuse to laugh and get release.

A priest in black with a cross poky face came in to shush us. Gina bundled her husband back into his seat.

16. Appearances and Disappearances

As the sniggers accompanying Enrico Lucellini's outburst had rippled around the congregation, Maria went all shamed and shy. And she hid behind me burying her head under my pullover. I could feel her sobbing.

Soon after this though servers began to busy themselves around the altar and two men opened the main doors wide. I touched my sister and whispered, *I think, I think he must be about to come in.*

Her head pushed out from under my arm, she had my hand in both of hers. With a sudden movement she rubbed her face in my pullover to brush away tears. She wouldn't let go of me not even to wipe her reddened eyes.

Through the great west door three boys entered, one holding up a crucifix, behind them came the Cardinal leading the remainder of his entourage.

We were expecting to behold a prince instead we saw an old man who looked as if he needed help to stay upright. He put one foot deliberately in front of the other. His head nodded and this made his mitre wave back and forth. It was hard to say if the nodding was done to acknowledge the people or because his neck needed a support collar.

He moved slowly up through the building. When he got near to where we were standing he stopped and peered through thick lenses at us.

My sister disappeared under the back of my pullover again. He shuffled towards me. A stifling sensation tightened round my throat. Maybe, maybe someone had told him what Maria had said, maybe ... I felt him take my left wrist. His bony forefinger was stroking the back of my hand.

My hand limp and lifeless in his. Somehow I knew he was smiling but I couldn't take my eyes away from his richly embroidered vestments.

He released my hand and moved on. I felt as if I were about to faint. The roof of the nave seemed to start revolving. If Maria hadn't been behind to hold me up I'd have collapsed for sure. An instant later though I came back to myself and in that moment distinctly saw the Cardinal put his embroidered shoe on Gina Lucellini's pink-dyed turkey feather.

Then something startled me. A nun, thin and tall with glasses, moved quickly over to the Cardinal touched the hem of his garments then retreated behind his accompanying party as this passed down the nave. She had reminded me of ... my heart jammed then began beating so berserkly it felt like it might somersault out of my chest.

Mother drew us back into our seats, me glancing wildly about in an effort to catch another glimpse of the thin nun.

She was nowhere to be seen.

My recollections of the Mass were vague. Maria spent more or less the whole time under my sweater. Having given up trying to get her to emerge. Mother didn't look at us again during the remainder of the service.

Neither she nor the Lucellinis took the Sacrament.

17. Preference

The Lucellinis made their way out almost before the service ended. But mother waited until the bulk of the people were moving toward the door before she marched out of the church leaving us to follow by ourselves. We were surrounded by the jackets and the shoes of grown ups. My sister pulled my arm to her as we slowly made our way along. Bright sunlight met us in the doorway. Mother stood stern faced near the bottom of the steps. We were about halfway down when she walked off without looking back. We followed reluctantly.

A little away from any groups of people on the space in front of the cathedral she turned round on us, *How could you? How could you shame me by asking if the Cardinal had brought a woman with him, how could you?*

The complaint was aimed more at my sister I guess but mother wasn't really looking at her. We made no attempt to answer. Maria's eyes filled with water.

Suddenly Gina appeared and taking mother by the arm pulled her away, *Martina cara, don't be too hard on them. They are only children.* She jerked round pointing with her thumb back at her husband, *But him! He is old enough to know better!* She screwed her eyes up making daggers shoot at him. Standing a little behind us Enrico made his face into a most sorrowful pout.

The women strode off. Still holding on mother's arm Gina Lucellini began to make her accented English purr.

As her husband passed by us he bowed down a bit, an Enrico smirk sneaking into his otherwise so pitiful appearance as he whispered, *They say the Cardinal prefers men.*

18. Back to the Bus

The meeting we had so waited for had come … and gone. The image I'd earlier conjured up of a church prince had paled even before we saw the Cardinal. But Maria had only Enrico Lucellini's laughter and my sweater to soften the suddenness of her fairytale Prince of the Church spelled out as an old nodding man.

Like a Hindu wife Enrico walked a couple of paces behind his spouse. Side by side we two followed more or less in their direction without speaking. Maria did a fair share of sniffling and eye drying.

The two women were talking near the bus, Enrico standing a yard behind his wife's back, mother keeping an eye on us. We were a little way off and mooching around, neither of us I guess felt much like getting back to the coach and the grown ups.

I think I saw M66.

Maria gasped. For a second a look of panic stole across her but then she clenched her fists, set her right foot forward and biting her lip put on one mean mug, *Did you really see that snake?*

Maybe.

We cast glances around the car park. I found myself shivering in spite of the sunshine.

Shall we go-
Back to the bus?

We nodded and ran off toward the coach.

19. Confessing

Maybe mother could tell you about a lot of things but it seemed clear that if we sought answers to hard questions like whether priests can have secret princesses or if Princes of the Church need staffs to lean on and neck support collars or ... well, she just wasn't the one to ask.

We wrote her a note: "Gon to confeshen".

I put it down on the edge of the kitchen table and we hurried off.

We were standing on the steps of the church dithering. The door swung open, Father Rufus appeared giving us a surprise.

We've, I sort of gulped, *We've, er, come to confess.*

Ah ah! And what have you got on your chests?

I looked down at my coat then over at my sister's.

He lifted one eyebrow and gave us an enquiring smile, *What do you want to confess?*

Maria blurted out, *We want to confess that we've got a lot of questions.* And we started asking one after the other.

We want to confess if priests have princesses.
And if card-in-halls are princes of the church.
And if they are, do they have princesses?
And do they lock them in high towers?
So they can prefer men?

He stepped back as though one had gotten in below the belt. But his expression changed to merriment when he saw how earnest we were. He nodded and managed to put on an air of gravity as he spoke, *Such profound problems need to be nourished. How do cookies and milk grab you?*

Maria looked stunned, *Shouldn't we confess in the confessional?*

Not about questions, questions aren't wrongdoings.

In the kitchen he poured out two glasses of milk and gave us each plate with a couple of cookies. Then he sat down with us at the smallish circular kitchen table covered with a white cotton cloth. He had a glass of water.

I don't know about cookies-grabbin-you but my fingers were itching to grab a cookie.

Maria gave him a reproachful look, *Aren't you going to eat some with us?*

He laughed, *I can see you aren't your mother's daughter for nothing!*

Getting up he put a cookie on a plate for himself. We all tucked in.

Hmm, let's see, what is your first question?

We wanted to know if you-, crumbs were spraying out of my mouth.

No! exclaimed Maria as she shot me a real anxious grown-up warning frown.

Father Rufus tilted his head from one to the other of us. I tried again without crumbs, *We thought somebody had lost something.*

And we wanted to find out what he'd lost.

And if Bibles are same.

Father Jerome's Bible didn't have any pictures, as my sister said this, she sort of slid halfway down the back of the chair, herself a picture of hopelessness.

But Maria says she can see pictures in your Bible and-

She transformed as I spoke as though afraid I was going to tell on her and cut me off, *But we don't know what he lost and, and it might have been a brother and, and,* her watery eyes glanced over to me.

That's right, she's right, we don't know what he lost but, but, my mouth couldn't seem to come up with anything but 'but'.

Father Rufus rubbed his forehead, *Hmm, let's try again. Not your first question, lets see, what's your most important question?*

Maria screwed up her face as though daring herself to dare to ask, *We want to know if a priest can have a princess?* Having said it she closed her eyes and held her breath.

Father Rufus seemed to have forgotten about breathing too. This somehow encouraged me to forget my stutter 'buts', *And if card-an-alls are Princes of the Church?*

They both looked at me and began to breathe again. I trailed off. My turn to slide down in the chair, *And why do they have cold hands? And what did Mr Lucellini mean about preferring men?*

I kind of mumbled this last to myself and as I did, I could see the Cardinal's robes. Almost against my will my eyesight, (my imaginary eyesight) was moving up his rich priestly vestments only, only when I came to face his smile, it wasn't him, it was M66!

It could chill a child to the marrow to see her scowl but her icy smile could probably bring on heart attacks to all and sundry. I shuddered violently.

They were still looking at me. *Can I sit by my sister?*

I got up and pushed my chair over to hers. We sat so as to lean our shoulders against each other.

Father Rufus stood up thoughtfully, filled our glasses and put another fat cookie on our plates, *Let me see if I can find an answer. In olden days, when fairytale was nearer to us than it is today, there were princes. There were princes and there were Princes. There were kings, princes, dukes, barons who ruled countries and regions. They looked after people, made and enforced laws and so on. But there were also other princes who outwardly might have been woodcutters', carpenters' or fishermen's sons – but they were real Princes who went on adventures and undertook quests. You know what quests are?*

We nodded. Mother had read us plenty of stories.

Well, the Church has governors to look after the people. These princes of the Church are called cardinals and they have their officers, bishops and priests and so on, to help them.

If I'd been listening as a grown-up I'd probably have muttered, "Organisation men".

He went on, *But there are also Princes of the Church who go on adventures, who undertake daring quests to distant realms, who bring back gifts, healing, renewal and messages to us. And just as the woodcutter, who went on an adventure in the fairytale, might never have been known to history so the deeds of certain Princes of the Church might not be known to any save the angels.*

He paused and playfully scrutinised our faces, *Do you know what such Princes of the Church are called?*

We shook our heads.

They are called saints.

We repeated the words. We loved to hear stories about saints. Maria went starry-eyed and said it once again to herself.

Will we ever see any Prince-Saints? I sure wanted to meet a real Church Prince and not one with cold fleshless fingers.

Father Rufus pursed his lips, *Well, they don't seem to be as common as they used to be. But you never know, Ray, you might be privileged to meet one some day.*

He sent a sharp glance at my sister.

Are they young? My mind was still on the Cardinal's bony cold finger.

He laughed, *Young, old, men, women, monks, nuns, bishops, lay folk, that is ordinary people, and even a parish priest or two. They come in all shapes and sizes. You can't recognise them by any obvious outer signs.*

But the angels know who they are? Maria was so serious as she spoke.

He set his jaw, *Yes, the angels know.*

You mean you could pass one by and never know it?

He turned to me as I spoke. *I think Ray, if you met a saint and you kept alert then you'd feel a deeper spiritual quality emanating from them, a joy or release after you left them perhaps and an incense of goodness in their presence. The French have a phrase: 'the perfume of sanctity'.*

'Emanating' was a tough word but incense I could get hold of that. Funny how when you're young, you sort of latch onto something and make a picture of the rest. To smell goodness – wow! What would a saint smell like?

My mind was wandering ... Marco Ammaretti's new dog, the kind which can snuffle out truffles. I was wondering if you could train it to smell out saints, and I began to imagine me and Marco in a big cathedral full of people with us holding the leash of a newly trained saint-sniffing butch. It let out a hound-dog howl as it scented a saint and began dragging us along crowded pews.

But do Prince-Saints have princesses? My sister still sounded pretty serious.

Father Rufus grinned, *What tenacity!*

I began to wonder if you could teach dogs to smell tenacity.

Let me tell you about a Prince-Saint from Central Italy, Umbria, a long time ago-

Maria interrupted him, *If there are women saints then there must be Princesses of the Church?*

His eyes twinkled, putting his finger to his lips he nodded and whispered, *But don't go telling anyone!*

Then he sat down and said softly to himself, *Assisi.* Closing his eyes for a moment before gazing out of the window. It was very quiet, the light was fading. We waited expectantly for a story. But he sighed and under his breath and murmured, *Chiara Lucia.*

What?

Oh, just someone I once knew.

Maria and me looked at each other. We didn't need to say anything.

Maybe losing the thread, Father Rufus stirred himself, *What did you mean about seeing pictures in my Bible?*

Maria spoke up, *Your Bible has got pictures. When you read about Peter last Sunday. I could see him. I can see him so clearly.*

I wasn't to be outdone, *I can see him too. He's got fuzzy black hair like Peter Mason's.*

He has not! Maria jumped up from the chair, *He hasn't, He hasn't!*

Her expression somewhere between being offended and being angry, and her foot was stamping out the difference.

Whoooah! He put a hand up to halt our argument hiding a smile under his frown. He went over and switched on the light. It was really getting dark. I glanced over at my sister ... dark ... mother!

Your mother does know you're here? As if reading my thoughts. Now it was his turn to look anxious, *We must get you back at once.*

Just then there was a knock on the door. He opened it. Mother with scarf over her head took a step in, *Why there you are, you little-* she stopped and cast Father Rufus a shy smiling sideways glance. *I looked everywhere for them. Till I found their note hanging up on the floor under the kitchen table.*

We were coming back through the woods when I came to a sudden realisation: If the Card-in-all's princess was a nun like M66 ... it was no wonder he preferred men.

... to be continued ...

Appendix

Dream Choices

When his daytime senses finally drowsed off dreams came, at first very disordered then far from pleasant ...

He is on the way to some place he can't quite remember when he notices a pancake house, goes in and stands watching the cook spreading pancake mixture in a hot pan. The warm smell of food and freshly ground coffee. He sits down with a double espresso and a couple of pancakes steeped in maple syrup.

The door is suddenly kicked open by some nut with a droopy Mexican moustache and white overalls full of pockets, in each pocket is a can of spray paint. With a canister of paint in each hand he bursts in squirting. Customers scream. He sprays graffiti on the walls, the floor and the backs of those in the café as they flee. The cook disappears by a back door.

Mineral turpentine mingles with smells of coffee and pancakes. Enrico is hoping to remain inconspicuous and sit through the commotion. Everyone else leaves, only he and the Crazed One remain. The Crazed notices him, lets out hysterical laughter and sidles toward him still with spray paint in either hand.

With a little self-conscious smile Enrico gestures politely as though inviting the Mad One to share his meal. The response: one pancake sprayed green, the other dripping with purple.

To his great surprise Enrico discovers his own voice sounds foreign when he tries to speak. He's taken on a toffee-nosed snobby English accent, *Well actually old boy, I'm not at all in favour of additives in food. Colourings in larger concentration have been known to produce adverse side-effects especially in persons of allergic disposition. With all due respect therefore may I propose ...*

His speech is cut short by another bout of maniacal giggling. Tossing away the paint cans the Crazed pushes his face closer toward Enrico who nervously touches his own upper lip and discovers he too has sprouted a moustache, one of the long thick twirling variety. El Loco carefully and clinically draws two more cans from his pocket. He aims, presses and one half of Enrico's Gay-Hussar moustache becomes tarry black, spray from the second can and the other half is white.

Feeling he has to play for time, Enrico pulls a large comb from his inside pocket and tries to comb his twirling whiskers. *Em, rather like treacle, I'm afraid to say.* The comb sticks fast, Enrico tugs at it nervously with both hands but can't get it loose. The whiskers extend more than a foot on either side of his face. The comb hangs like a decoration on a branch of a Christmas tree. *Actually, back in the Old Country only ladies and of course gents in the acting profession take recourse to make-up.*

The Crazed squints at him.

I say, old boy, you don't happen to have a brush on you by any chance?

The Crazed lets out a pained and animal like cry as he hurls the cans toward the kitchen area. They burst into flame. The smell of burning paint fills the room. Enrico's stomach turns over, he wants to throw up. El Loco viciously kicks over the table between them and stands legs a little apart, hands above a pair of holsters. And in the holsters guns, spray paint guns. About two paces separate them.

Enrico, making movements reminiscent of a frog before it croaks, is unable to keep it back any longer. A stream of puke spews out of him and takes El Loco in the chest with the force of a fire jet knocking him over backwards. Cans of paint spill from his pockets all over the restaurant floor.

For a short while a wonderful sense of relief comes over Enrico. Then his nostrils detect the stench of vomit. Puke inside and outside begins to overwhelm his consciousness.

Something cold presses against his brow. Opening his eyes he sees aimed at his forehead and now about two inches away a rifle, a pain-spraying rifle.

"I'll be marked for life", thinks Enrico without the slightest fear or suspense.

High-pitched yet muffled laughter as the Crazed draws the spray-gun back about a foot and ... presses the trigger.

Jasmine.

The heavy overpowering scent of jasmine. The canister is filled with cheap perfume: Jasmine with an after smell of athlete's foot.

Suffocation comes over Enrico. He staggers to his feet and makes a break for the door. El Loco is after him, drenching him from tip to toe in the perfume. Enrico steps on a spray canister a biggish one. His legs run as fast as pistons but he isn't moving forward. The canister has become huge and is turning on the spot as he tries to run on it.

The Crazy One jubilantly dances around spraying him. In a last attempt to make a getaway Enrico lunges forward and lands on the hard floor. He lies there unable to budge. Heavy footsteps approach. El Loco kneels beside him and mutters, *Ah, ah, poor one!*

Then he begins to touch up Enrico's monk-cut like a would be barber. Fearing the worst Enrico engages every effort of his will to try to move, every fibre in his body strains. He manages a slow-motion crawl.

El Loco takes out another can of spray and presses: Foam, creamy white foam with the consistency of soft ice squirts onto Enrico's bald top. With one hand the Crazed holds the can and with unhurried movements of the other he moulds the form of the viscous foam. Enrico can feel a gooey helmet sticking to his head as he creeps desperately and yet so slowly toward the exit.

The Crazed stands up and squirts excitedly. From his reflection in the glass door Enrico sees two blobs like large soft ices appearing on his goo-covered head. El Loco works feverishly on the blobs to transform them. They become ... ears ... giant white rabbit ears sticking up from his goo helm.

Enrico strains to reach up to the door handle, opens the door, a draught of fresh breeze, freedom to move, to stand. Joyfully running down the steps, there are many more on the descent than he remembers when entering the café, white marble steps like those before a monument. Halfway down, he turns back to see the Crazed on top of the steps with a canister crying out, *El Locissimo!* He presses, thick choking fumes gush forth.

The Crazed is engulfed by smoke.

Enrico flees down the steps to escape the noxious gases.

He remembers as he runs that he ought to be going somewhere and he's late.

At the bottom of the steps is a taxi with its engine running. Dark clouds splutter from its exhaust. Enrico closes his mouth, holds his breath, opens the taxi door and dives in, only to find himself lying on his back on the sidewalk. When trying to get in he thrust the rabbit ears against the roof of the cab but having become so rubbery they rebounded causing him to be flung backwards. Luckily gelled goo protects the back of his head which is now bouncing up and down, up and down, like a ball as he lies there.

Another attempt to enter, ducking this time. Still no way in. The Gay Hussar is too wide. El Loco's paint has hardened and the moustache scrapes and knocks against the doors.

With great effort: twisting, bending, turning, he manages to get in. And once in, he tries to sit but the ears stick up too high. He half leans, half sprawls on the back seat.

Okay where to, buddy? The accent might have been from the Bronx. The driver is motionless. Enrico can only see his back.

Take me to ... he cannot remember his intended destination, he's completely forgotten, so he tries to make polite conversation, *Er, lovely weather we're having.*

Ten degrees of frost!

Oh, yes of course, cold enough to freeze the balls off brass monkeys and all that. Enrico just can't believe its him that's doing the snooty speak.

The driver twists slightly and blows out smoke. The scent of cigarettes reminds Enrico of his youth in Naples.

Absent mindedly thinking back to how they used to wolf whistle after the girls, *The wenches had such fleshy buxom behinds!* He intended to use an Italian expression of similar meaning.

Wha? Cut the crap, Mac! Where to, where yer wanna go?

Enrico closes the taxi door, urgently trying to figure out which city he is in.

The, the, to the ... to Westminster Abbey, yes to Westminster.

Wha!? The driver turns sideways as he speaks.

Enrico's heart misses a beat, this guy too has a moustache; could he be the Crazed ducking up again in disguise?

The driver sniffs, *Say, yer got a broad back there?*

The nauseous smell of foot-enriched jasmine filling the vehicle is even beginning to overcome its wearer.

The driver coughs violently and turns to face Enrico the Rabbit-eared, *What a stink! Get out of my cab you dirty ra-, yer dirty rabbit.*

The driver jumps out, opens one of the back doors and pulls Enrico out by the ears, the false ones. The huge Gay Hussar moustache sticks fast in the doorway. Pushing, pulling and with his foot pressing against the taxi, the driver finally manages to drag out his would-be passenger.

Angrily shouting to someone across the street as he gets back in and drives off.

A Kung-Fu kid comes running up, he jerks Enrico up by the jacket and lets him have it. A kick to the stomach, a chop across the chest, Enrico bows under a succession of blows. Somehow they don't really hurt him, only numb him. Ranting incomprehensibly the kid lifts his karate hand and puts his face threateningly close to Enrico's.

Look here matey is all this fuss so awfully necessary? Enrico is stopped in mid sentence as the Kung-Fu kid lets out a karate roar and, with his whole body behind it, brings a chop right down between the rabbit ears. The blow would sure have split a beam or broken tiles piled one upon the other. Enrico sinks to his knees under the impact.

But the Kung Fu kid's chopping arm flies upwards. The rebound from the goo helm has such force that it takes his whole body upwards into a somersault nearly ten feet about ground. The kid lands in a crumpled heap in front of Enrico moaning in that same outlandish lingo.

It's time you foreign blighters learnt the King's English. Enrico's accent still as snootily posh as before. This clown kid of Kung Fu cries like a baby as he holds up a now deformed chopping arm.

Enrico begins to feel a bit sorry for him, *Look here old chap no real harm done, you know.*

He gets no further, his erstwhile adversary's eyes glaze over, the jasmine has taken away his senses. He slumps at Enrico's feet. The perfume even starts to make its wearer swoon until Kung Fu practitioners in all shapes and sizes crowd around Enrico whooping and screeching.

One tries to chop him across the face but Enrico weaves his head away and the chop lands on the Gay Hussar. The hand of his attacker breaks with a sharp snapping sound.

Another kid kicks at his head, again Enrico bobs away, again he takes it on the Hussar and there's another crack of breaking bone, another Kung-Fu kid wails.

A third chops him from behind across the back of the goo helmet. The rebound sends the kid pirouetting, spinning like a top and flattening many of the attackers in the process. In the pandemonium Enrico makes a dash for it. With Kung Fu shrieks in his ears, he runs and runs.

His mode of running hardly deserves to be termed athletic, more like that of a pig farmer in galoshes tramping through slop. *Knees up, knees up*, pants Enrico to encourage himself.

The shouts of his assailants lessen and fade. At last he dares to turn back. He's only moved away a few yards but the Kung Fu clan all seem to have shrunk to doll size. He waves back to them, *Must be on my way. Knees up, knees up*, he puffs and blows as he runs energetically on the spot.

A bus! A bus by the curb and just about to pull away. Enrico jumps on. The driver motions with his head for him to go further inside. Enrico is beaming as he makes his way down the gangway. Here is warmth and – and grannies!

The bus is full of grannies. Almost identical grannies with glasses, poking noses, backs slightly hunched, dark clothing and black umbrellas. All are eyeing him aggressively. Enrico's open-hearted smile drains away to self-conscious facial twitches.

A musty, crusty old people's smell hangs in the vehicle. The grannies rise from their seats jeering and threatening him with their umbrellas.

Swineherd!
Rabbiter!
Swelterer!
Scenty stinker!
Vomitter!

Arsonist!
Painter!

The appellations seem somehow valid for his nostrils. He registers the smell of pigsties, troughs, rotting fur, foot-enriched perfume, burning paint. His Gay Hussar moustache seems to have become tacky and tarry again.

The aggression is no longer verbal. He is jostled then attacked with umbrellas. Thwack, he is being poked and struck.

Get him!
Give it to him!

The grannies are roaring. The driver jams on the brakes. Enrico shoots forward in the bus landing on his back, grannies pile up on top of him.

Crushed, trodden on, pushed, pulled, thumped, jabbed and then finally he is tossed off the coach.

As it drives off he can see grannies crowding at the windows, giving him the finger.

He tries to get up but discovers his arms are stuck fast to the twirling Hussar and he only succeeds in rolling over. He lies huddled in the gutter, freezing asphalt under him.

How many times did the goo-helmeted one seek to rise and yet each time the weight of the whiskers toppled him. At last in wrath he rips his sleeves free and rises. Standing triumphant as a hero: Tattered sleeves, giant rabbit ears and a couple of granny umbrellas stuck by their handles to either side of his now hardening Hussar moustache.

A smart notion strikes him, the subway! Go down a subway station, find out where he is and perhaps then he'll remember where he wants to go.

Reasoning it would be quicker to fly, he leaps hoping to glide on the Hussar. He comes down, jumps again, the umbrellas open behind him. Up, down, such good fun, springing like a kanga and crying out, *Enrico the roo!*

Suddenly the ground is gone from under his feet. Falling, down, down then with a jolt he hits the hard concrete of a subway station.

At this point he almost wakes up, sensing that he is lying in his own bedroom ... but dream overpowers him again.

Artificial ventilation blowing stale air up from subway depths. Smells of a station below the surface. People about him, nameless hurrying figures in the thrall of rush-hour mania. Expressionless normality bumps and jostles him. He notices a free escalator and turning sideways so his Hussar and the attached umbrellas take up less space, he inches toward it. He gains the top and as if on a spirited steed he charges down.

Running quickly down but moving slowly because the escalator is climbing upwards. At last he reaches the floor below panting.

Dimmer lighting, staler air, no posters, maps or signs, no more people. Turning a corner he comes to a long flight of descending stairs. One shortish, middle-aged Afro guy walks past him rolling the whites of his eyes and pointing fearfully down the descending steps as he speaks, *Disused man, disused!*

He rushes away in the direction Enrico came from. Enrico is standing alone but feels his pride pricked.

Was he speaking to me? Am I disused or am I used. Used or disused, that is the question.

He chuffs himself up and declaims aloud in learnèd tones, *Academician Enrico, used or disused? If I am disused then I am not used. And if I am not used then in acting I must use. And if I use then I am not disused. Therefore I am disused and not disused. And being both am and not, am therefore everything and can do anything!*

Proudly puffing himself up even more, *This is the start of the Academy of Enrico!* He begins to skip down the steps.

Enricetto, the woman's voice calling to him sounds melodious and so familiar, so very familiar.

He turns back. A little above him at the top of the steps stands a woman dressed as a Red Indian. She is young, maidenly, beautiful, kind.

Enrico knows he knows her – but from where?

Shy as a child and feeling lonely he wants only to run to her. He wants her to tickle him, take off his rabbit-eared helmet and his Hussar, change his diaper.

Blushing. Has he dirtied his pants? Hoping she doesn't notice he surreptitiously feels with his hand around his ass. Sniffing – good, no pooh-pooh smells.

From her clothing he detects scents of woodlands, of wild forest, of winds, mountains, flowers, prairies, oceans. Stars are embroidered on her dress. Ineffable yearnings arise in his heart, *Are you my mother?*

She smiles tearfully, *I mothered your mother before your father was born.*

Enrico's heart misses a beat is she, could she be – a granny ... he looks but, thankfully, he can see no umbrellas on her.

Are you ...

No Enrico, I know your question before you ask. I am she who knows you better than you know yourself. I sang to you before your birth.

Tears well from his inmost being, he reaches out blindly toward her. But she continues almost as if scolding him, *Beware, Enrico, of becoming haughty, of displaying plumes, of falling, of addiction and of rotting.*

At this juncture another thought begins to whisper in him, that he is a grown man, not a little kid with a dirty diaper and far too important a person to learn from squaws in disused subways.

I'm sorry Miss, mi dispiace signorina ma- His own voice, his own, not snooty speak! *Io, io sono,* he shouts loudly, *I, me, mine, am,* and with hardly another thought skips down the stairs.

Floating on a blast of stale air which blew up and opened the umbrellas on his Hussar. He drifts on them. The upward movement of air slows his fall. Floating down, twirling, falling. With a bump he reaches the next level down and glances back up.

No one is there. No Indian maid kindly and lovely, no one. Her absence cuts him to the quick. He pouts like a baby.

But soon something else gets control of him again, *Huh, after all I am a grown man with a rabbit helmet. And my Hussar moustache with its four umbrellas must surely signify self possession.* Demonstratively he fastens the umbrellas and marches down the tunnel.

The only sounds, his own footsteps and the clinking of umbrellas on the Hussar.

An age seems to go by. One tunnel then another finishes in a dead end or in the rubble. He is completely lost. The lighting grows ever dimmer.

Scraping sounds, something scurries over his feet. He strikes a match and makes out a rat-like shape. To his surprise light from the match not only allows his sense of sight to function but strangely enlivens his olfactory organs. Jasmine, heavy artificial jasmine.

Rats scamper away choked by the perfume. Enrico feels the conceit of a one who is able to repel rats, rise up in him. He mutters proudly, *A mature man with goo ears and a Hussar who repels rats in disused subways.*

The last phrase disconcerts him, makes him aware that he is underground and lost.

Scratchings and scurrying, vermin fleeing from his exotic olfactory aura.

He lights matches one after another just to allow his sense of smell to awaken. He is moaning softly as he strikes, *Jasmine, oh jasmine my addiction.* Reaching up as though to take tactile hold of the perfume, his hand clasps only an umbrella.

Darkness. Deprived both visual and nasal input. Only faint scratching sounds and unfulfilled longings for jasmine.

One match left.

Fear.

Fear of life sans light, sans scents … only dark, dust and dull, sexless scrapings.

The last match is a whopper, the size of a short pencil. Further down the tunnel he notices it is less dark. Moving forward hopefully, yet still holding tightly to the match. Enough natural light to make out tunnel walls. He is standing under a shaft. Far above is a circular opening.

Daylight, he whispers poignantly as another Enrico seems to arise within him, one who remembers life on the outside with winds, skies, people, childhood, laughter and restful sleep, and who dearly wishes to be freed from disused subway tunnels and burnt-out nerve endings.

A ladder, a rusted iron ladder runs up the side of the shaft. He puts his foot on a rung and holding on with his left hand begins to climb.

When he reaches up with his right hand he realises he still holds the match, the thickness of a candle. This seems to throb in his grip and grow to dynamite size. An inner struggle arises in him: to let go and choose day life and freedom above or to strike and fill his breast with forbidden odour and perhaps pass away in narcotic revelry. To strike or not to strike: his arm shakes, his body trembles. In an effort to break free from the conflict he jerks his hand violently down. Whether this is in attempt to throw away or strike the match he knows not which. The match-head scrapes against the wall. Friction sets it ablaze with the brilliance of burning magnesium. Even through closed eyelids the light pierces him.

The dazzle is short-lived and dulls to a ruddy flame. Cheap perfume wafts with the smoke, ash falls to the tunnel floor. Beneath him is movement. Crawling from cracks in the concrete are little rodents the size of large mice. One stands on its hind legs and sniffs the air. Enrico notices that where its eyes should be are only indentations, it is blind. Its head hardly more than a pug nose and gaping nostrils. With a thrill and a tingling sensation spreading through him, he recognises the creature. In childhood he was fascinated by mythological animals especially those in the Bestiary of Leoangelico, drawings of legendary creatures by the famed Renaissance artist. And now there before his very (dreaming) eyes is a snifrotter or snuffledear.

Not one but many, a hundred or more perhaps. According to the Bestiary: Snifrotters are rodent-like animals whose only nutrients are smells and stinks. They live in hordes and on encountering a living creature stick to it like leeches with their six nostrils and suck. They suck away all its scent, leaving their victim paralysed, lifeless.

Fearsome indeed is death by snifrotting.

Enrico can see they have already localised the source of perfume with their snorting pugs and are beginning to crawl up the ladder. He realises his only hope is to move away – fast! He starts to climb again in earnest. His legs and left hand function well but he cannot bring himself to let go of the match. It burns slowly and with its smoke wafts ravishing Jasmine.

He makes his faltering way up the ladder using his right elbow instead of his right hand. Not far beneath him are snifrotters. Just being near the Jasmine energises the creatures into a frenzy.

Half way up and tiring. Only a rung or two separates him from the horde of snifrotters surging up from below.

Maybe old stories are false. Maybe death by snifrotting ain't such a bad way to go.

The match glowing in his hand feels like purple marshmallow. The burning nears his fingers ... closer, hot, scorching ... before his eyes a blister appears on his hand. With a cry of rage and pain he lets go. The match twirls flickering down into darkness and lands with a shower of sparks.

Far below him Enrico can make out a circle of snuffledears around the match's glow. All of a sudden they attack, open nostrils going straight for the burn. A furious heaving of creatures. Darkness. From the depths comes the stink of singeing snifrotters. Ah, what foul stench is comparable to that of a burning snuffledear.

By sheer force of will Enrico drags his gaze from black depths and looks up. Daylight is closer. The wish to be free awakens anew. He makes a grab for the next rung with his elbow and slips.

Hanging on by the left hand, umbrellas knocking against steel. Somehow he gets his feet back on the ladder, squashing a few snifrotters in the process.

Now the creatures are swimming round his legs. Their nostril suckers sticking fast to his clothing.

Climbing quickly with both hands. As the snuffledears suck, they swell up like leeches.

Whether because of their weight or because they suck life as well as scents from him he cannot say but his movements become slow.

Close to the circular opening, only two or three more rungs and his rabbit ears will pop up. But paralysis is fast taking hold of his muscles. He is conscious of his head. Arms and legs are only crustaceans, foreign appendages to the brain. His brain pressing against the inside of his skull.

Snuffledears crowd on the umbrellas, on his Hussar moustache, even upon the goo helm, sucking, sucking.

The odour of heavy jasmine surrounds him, only to be vacuumed into ballooning lung-bellies of the snifrotters.

Then comes reeking vomit, burning paint smells. Fumes which crept and creep into his brain and make him conscious only of his head.

Anger, a righteous and passionate wrath flames in the breast of Enrico even to match the furry of snifrotters. Against all odds he will make the daylight.

His rabbit ears push up a little above the level of the road. The sound of thudding metal.

Darkness.

Enrico filled with desperation, has he got so far and with such toil only to be thwarted by someone putting a manhole cover over his escape route?

Enrico, the Desperado, heaves his head against the metal covering causing it to move. He rams the top of his head against it. Luckily the upper part of his goo helm is still intact not yet sucked into snuffledear lungs.

The manhole cover lifts, reaches the vertical and topples forwards. Enrico's helmet has become gooey again and sticks to the metal cover so when it falls, he is pulled up like a cork from a wine bottle. His arms pinned to his over-plump waist by the manhole. His body is doubled up with his helm stuck to the cover.

Two snufflers are on his head, their pug noses going at the goo helmet; they break its seal with the manhole cover. Enrico's torso springs upright and vibrates back and forth with the rebound.

Enrico is popping up from the manhole, arms pinned against his belly. The clothes on his upper body have disappeared, vacuumed perhaps into the snuffler-guts. His torso naked except for the hair on his chest.

His legs hang beneath the hole. Snuffler vermin cluster upon them.

At first the daylight is too bright for his eyes. After his eyes adjust, he sees people walking past him on a busy street. One trips over the manhole cover and swears.

Enrico feels acutely embarrassed to be sticking up there in the middle of a busy sidewalk with his upper body bare except for the remaining blob of the goo helm on his bald top and two snuffledears snufted fast to his head.

Nobody seems to take any notice of him. Should he cry for help or suffer in his modesty?

Then he realises the people are blind. They all wave sticks in front of them to detect obstacles.

An old lady pokes hers into Enrico's navel and walks around him measuring out his waistline with her stick.

To shout or not to shout?

Enrico's mind is made up when he feels how on his dangling legs snifrotters close upon his private parts.

Help, help! his voice has become a kind of high-pitched croaking. The thought even crosses his mind that his croaks might be above the audible spectrum of sound.

One passer-by stops, puts her pointed nose in the air and sniffs, *Jasmine?*

Another stops. Then another, then another. *Paint?*
Burning paint?
Fire?
Fire?
Fire! Fire! Fire!

Enrico's falsetto croaking joins their chorus. A blind fireman with a huge hose attached to a fire hydrant moves forwards checking the direction with his nose. The nozzle points straight at Enrico's stuck up torso.

No! gasps Enrico.

Out of the hose pours foam. Thick oozing foam. He still cannot shout.

Then as in a romantic movie his rescuer appears, Gina. *Hi, Enrico.* She gives him a big smile, a kiss and a clinch.

Don't spend too much time in the bubble bath darling. I'll be waiting for you. You gorgeous hunk of flesh! Oh and by the way, do take those fluffy muffs off your head before they get soaking wet.

She gives one of the snufflers a flick with her finger and turns to walk away giving Enrico a wriggle with her bottom and a naughty wave over her shoulder.

Gi, Gi, Gi, Enrico croaks then suddenly his full voice roars, *Ginaaa!*

But foam bubbles over his mouth, his nose. Beneath the road he can feel how the snuffledears have attained his private parts.

Closing his eyes as he disappears in the foam Enrico, the once Rabbit-eared, resolves to meet his further fate with equanimity.

He wakes ... to a dream within a dream.

In what looks like a large private room in a hospital Enrico is sitting up in bed dressed in an off-white smock. Three youths cross-legged on the floor are beside his bed.

As he glances at them they bow until their foreheads momentarily rest upon the chequered floor.

Eh! exclaims Enrico in surprise. In an instant one youth has grabbed pencil and paper, another slate and chalk, the third an unglazed vase and brush dripping ink.

Well, I'll be!

They write swiftly, calligraphic brush marks on the vase, runes on slate, words on paper. Enrico gets the strangest feeling they are writing down what he said.

The youths look at each other in wonder. Then one of them speaks, *Oh Enrico the Wise, your words carry such prophetic power. You have told us the future will bring well-being to yourself. And surely*, they all bow again, *Also to us, your humble disciples.*

As Enrico rubs his bald top in astonishment he notices a young man with monk-cut hair in the open doorway who is wearing a smock to match his own and who, like Enrico himself, is scratching his scalp.

He points at the man. The man points back.

What? mumbles Enrico.

The youths at his feet write on paper, slate, and vase. The man in the doorway makes a gesture of astonishment.

Enrico lifts an eyebrow, *Ah, Ah!*

The disciples whisper among themselves.

A riddle indeed.

A Koan?

I will repeat this day and night: *What? Ah, ah! What! Ah, ah! – surely this is a lifeline to the heights.*

An enigmatic smile steals over Enrico's face, he straightens his back and nods toward the man in the doorway his voice resounds in regal tones, *You speak.*

The man bows low and accompanies his speech with hand movements, *I – make – your – words – visible – for – the – deaf – even – they – shall – learn – your – wisdom, Oh, Wise – One.*

Enrico hears clicking sounds and glances over to a corner of the room where someone sits hunched up in front of some sort of electronic screen typing.

You, says Enrico sternly, *And your tube.*

The young man turns from the screen, straightens his glasses and addresses Enrico, *I am a nerd.*

A turd?

Brush strokes, scribbles, hand signs and whi*sperings.*

Is the Wise One indicating to us that nerds are turds?

With a big and apparently open smile the young man at the keyboard continues, *I push your maxims out onto the net. I am so to speak the gate. When the world wants to explore your words, they goggle at my window to the web.*

And the bill? Who pays the bill? mutters Enrico troubled.

A cent for me on every transaction!

Computer games, says Enrico shaking his head, *I prefer monopoly.*

The basic game I visualise.

Enrico shoos him away and turns to the boys on the floor, *Geek speak!*

Is the Wise One warning us against the Web?

Or of monopolies?

Or of speaking like geeks?

To think he already conceives the future of computer science!

Enrico is feeling peckish, *Cookies?*

The disciples write. Enrico murmurs something under his breath in Italian. The man in the doorway lifts an eyebrow and gestures toward the loins.

Nobody speaks. The only sound is the blower whirring in the computer.

Can't you put a net over that noise? asks Enrico.

Being personal? moans the nerd. *Blowing's necessary, your face filmed and overblown, as I pad around and advertise, and so make I great stores and advertise. The tube you goggle at becomes the 'S'; the 'S' with double lines, the apple of my eye.*

At this point the screen goes blank. The young man at the computer takes off his sandals and puts on boots.

Enrico longing for an espresso, *Coffee?*

Not from Indonesia, retorts the nerd in curt and surly fashion.

Well, how about a biscuit? Enrico trying to be conciliatory, *A Penguin chocolate biscuit perhaps?*

A strangled cry of rage comes from the geek, *I'm on my jobs, I won't give you sauce! You ain't gonna get free from me! A bite on my pear is meant to hook!*

A long and complicated dialogue ensues between Enrico and the nerd ... which will not be related here. Suffice it to say Enrico uses words in more or less their usual meanings while the greedy geek seems to be referring to a High-Tech world to which Enrico, a man living in the late Fifties, has no access. The contrast in their meaning-sets causes their diffuse talk to be carried rapidly and haphazardly along but the nerd always seeks to take over the direction of their dialogue and drive the conversation along on his own terms for his own ends and his own gain.

In the end though something upsets him and threatening Enrico with a lawsuit, he stamps across the room in hob-nob jackboots and climbs awkwardly out of the window.

Enrico shakes his head, he is left with the distinct impression that they were each talking within their own worlds.

The boys cross-legged on the floor are still making notes and replicating his dictations.

The computer's burring distracts Enrico, *Pull out the plug.*

To his further annoyance his audience only writes down what he says. He is about to mutter something under his breath when he notices the sign-language interpreter on the verge of making an indelicate gesture.

And disconnect! shouts Enrico vehemently.

Quietness. The sun shines in through half-open blinds. Enrico's mind wandering again to food, he glances over hopefully to the bedside table. Only a glass of water.

One of the disciples breaks the stillness, *Oh Wise One, we are not technocrats, tell us of Surrealism.*

Enrico leans back to rest in the posture of a Greek aesthete. *Intellectual and thereby only puerile attempts to make life in dreams meaningful to the day.*

They write with feverish excitement. A second disciple asks, *Tell us of Magic Realism.*

He's never heard of this, yet no matter, whatever he says, will be taken as replete with hidden significance.

Magic Realism is a morbid condition whereby its sufferers, being unable to distinguish fully between the dreaming and waking states, mistakenly speak of happenings possible only in dreams as though they were actual events in the external world.

More scribbling. About twenty vases are piled up on each other, two dozen slates, a couple notepads. The third disciple speaks, *Tell us, oh Sage, of angels.*

Enrico pulls his knees into him, misty depths and longings touch him, his eyes moisten. *Angels, mm, your angel is an Indian maid upon whose dress the stars of heaven shine, who sings to you before your birth, who seeks for you even in disused subways – and warns against ostrich hairstyles in the Fall.*

Enrico ponders what his own cryptic statements might imply. Then he notices the interpreter for the deaf making what could easily be construed as unsightly motions.

What would you wish?
Oh – Wise – One, I – am – in – need.
Of what?
Pain – is urging – me – not – to – forgo – urination.
Enrico nonchalantly tosses him the bedpan.

Unfortunately it has not been emptied. A pungent and altogether obnoxious odour fills the room. Enrico waves the interpreter away. Drenched and clutching the pan between his legs, he bows and hobbles out through the door.

Furtive whisperings among the disciples. They stand as they venture to ask in chorus, *Oh, tell us of fallen angels*.

Then they cringe and huddle together on the floor.

Enrico proudly protrudes his jaw and adopts the posture of an Indian brave at a Pow-Wow, *Let me your sitting chief explain-*

He gets no further. A bullish looking she-nurse enters and sends a stare at the three youths who rapidly excuse themselves, *Oh Wise One, forgive us but, well, you know how it is, we must away.*

Even before they make the exit, she pushes Enrico the Dreamwise down on his back, and draws from beneath her uniform a huge thermometer brandishing it before him, *Is the rammometer in store for this patient today?*

As she straightens up, he dives under the bedclothes.

He hears her chanting.

Anaesthesia, dementia, euthanasia, rammometer … Popping his bald top out from under the bedclothes, he is just up in time to see her spin a roulette wheel.

She rubs her hands, *Euthanasia, euthanasia, Eu – drat! It's Anaesthesia! It's the anaesthetics then for you.*

Enrico dives back under the clothes.

With a violent jerk of her hand, the she-nurse rips off all the bedclothes and menacingly bends over his prostrate form, *Shall we first de-smock?* She runs her eye up and down him as she touches the thick layer of make-up covering the stubble on her chin. Flexing a muscularity which might make an Olympic shot putter seem like an anorexia victim, she pins him on the bed with one hand and with the other pulls a mask over his face.

"Gas!" Enrico detects the sweet delusive smell of laughing gas. He tries to hold his breath.

With the delicacy of an all-in wrestler she starts to tickle him ... being overcome ... drifting ... away to ... the foam of the previous dream ... and further, further ...

He wakes up in their dark bedroom with a weight pressing on heavily on his chest.

His wife is lying across him in her gigantic hairnet.

The hairnet is causing his nostrils to itch.

Enrico's nights are at least as adventurous as his days.